BLOOD OF DEMONS

BOOK THREE OF THE CASTILLIAN BLOOD SERIES

KILLIAN WOLF

Grim House
Publishing

ISBN - 978-1-951140-06-9

Editor: Claerie Kavanaugh claeriekavanaugh.com/need-an-editor
Copyeditor: saltandsagebooks.com
Cover design: miblart.com
Formatter: Grim House Publishing LLC grimhousepub.com/plans-pricing

CONTENTS

Silence falls upon my cohorts as I stand front and center in the Reaper Council courtroom. Their hollow eyes glare back at me—the reaper who was turned human and killed by Azazel's hand. Everyone, including me, had expected me to be dead. But here I am, with my hood down, and in my human skin. But I am not human.

I shut my eyes, attempting to block out the chatter echoing through the room. Images of reapers and demons warring upon one another still flash across my memory. One minute, I was human, having gone through extreme temperatures in the Savannah desert, and then feeling the grief of losing my memory. The next, I was stabbed in the back and dying in my beloved girlfriend's arms, until she was pulled away by her brother to save her life. I squeeze my eyes tighter. *My poor Addison. Where are you?*

"Do you think this is some kind of evolution?" someone asks.

Someone else scoffs. "Evolution? This is an abomination. Reapers cannot fall in love with humans." The murmurs continue as I stand and wait patiently for Deacon to arrive.

A bony hand presses down gently on my shoulder. I open my eyes to Deacon's icy stare and then she gives me a nod. Her red bangs fall straight down to her cheeks. She's in human form as well. I nod back and follow her behind the podium where our late Judge's scythe lies flat.

Deacon grabs the gavel and bangs it on the table three times. The courtroom falls silent again.

"There is a reason why this council meets in a courtroom," Deacon begins. I take a few steps away from the podium, to let Deacon have her dramatic introduction. I'm tired of being the focus of attention. I stare at her with the rest of the reapers. She raises her hood over her head as her eyes sink back into their sockets, leaving only the hollow gaze of a skull. Her skin dissipates as her skeletal figure emerges.

"We make decisions for not only our council, and for humankind, but also for the entirety of LLAPS." She pauses and glimpses at the audience of reapers. Some are sitting with arms crossed, others tapping their feet anxiously.

"Last night we joined together in hand-to-hand combat against Azazel and his league. We did something that hadn't been done in a millennium since our late Judge sentenced Azazel himself to the cages."

"What about Lucifer?" someone calls out. Deacon holds out her hand.

"Lucifer will be found and dealt with."

"What do we do now without the Judge?" someone else says.

"Yeah, who is going to give the orders with him gone?" says another.

Deacon hits the gavel on the podium. "Please, I know

you have many questions, and I will try my best to answer them. As you all know, I have been the Judge's right-hand reaper for hundreds of years. I see it suiting that I take up his scythe and continue his work as Judge. Does anyone object?"

Silence spreads among them as they all look at one another.

I mean obviously, who else would it be? This is what he has been training her for. I lift my hands to clap.

"Hold on." A voice comes from the far end of the courtroom.

Deacon furrows a brow bone. "Yes? Uhh . . . Lorcan?"

I resist the urge to roll my eyes. Lorcan has always had opposing opinions when it suits him but pretends to be on par with all of reaper law. He's had it out for me since even before I went after Abyzou. Lorcan stands up from the end and points to me. Great, here it comes. "How did he come back to life? And is he still human?"

I scowl at Lorcan. All the other reapers stare me down. I shoot a look at Deacon and then back to the audience. I open my mouth, but Deacon cuts me off.

"Right. Under the hand of Azazel, Ambrose was turned human, only to be killed in battle after he had come back to aid us. But—I noticed he wasn't dead yet. But dying. I returned him to the Akashic waters where he was rejuvenated back to himself."

"Back to himself? So then, as reaper?"

"I'll answer that, Deacon." I take a few steps forward and peer through the audience until my eyes meet with Lorcan's. "Yes, Lorcan, I am back to being a reaper."

Lorcan curls his lips, locking his eyes with me as he speaks. "Well then, I suppose we have you to thank, Deacon, for saving one of our fellow . . . brothers." His gaze finally frees mine and turns to all the others. "I would not be opposed to following Deacon in our late Judge's place." Lorcan darts his eyes back to mine one more time before sitting back down, and I quirk an eyebrow in return.

"Any other questions?" Deacon asks.

Someone else stands up. "After it all happened, some of us still don't have our scythes."

"Ah yes, I have collected the scythes that Azazel had confiscated and will return them to all of you right after this meeting is adjourned."

The council claps.

"In that case," Deacon raises her voice, "with the power of myself and this council of Reapers I declare myself Judge of the Reaper Council." Deacon straightens her back and the council grows silent, in anticipation of Deacon grabbing the scythe.

I smile as I watch Deacon place her hand on the hilt, slowly taking in the moment. If there was ever a reaper who was a rule-following servant to the order, it was Deacon. She's going to make a fine Judge. I wonder who she'll have as her right hand.

A red, burning light washes over the courtroom. Deacon shouts as she's flung into the wall. Angry welts rise on her hand. Members of the council stand, jaws dropped. The Judge's golden scythe is about to hit the ground. I leap through the air to keep it from hitting the floor, not thinking about the possible repercussions.

The scythe lands perfectly in my hand. And as it hits, I wince, expecting it to sear my palm the way it did hers. Instead, it glows a bright, powerful blue that lights up my face. The energy from the scythe pulses through my body, lifting me up. My human skin sinks deep into my bones, revealing my hollowed eyes and sleek mandible. The court-room gasps and watches in horror.

Deacon pushes up and steps forward, in awe. She clears her throat. "It looks as though the scythe has chosen its owner instead."

All eyes are on me as I come down to my feet. My eyes never leave the scythe and my lips part, shock reverberating through my bones.

"This has to be a mistake," I sputter out. "I can't be the Judge."

Lorcan vaults to his feet, sending his chair clattering to the floor. "Absolutely not. I refuse to follow a reaper who fell in *love* with a human. He's broken every rule in the book! Do we not all agree?"

The courtroom erupts into protests.

"Agree or disagree!" Deacon bangs the gavel on the podium as she collects herself from having hit the wall. "Perhaps Ambrose's experiences have caused the Judge's scythe to choose him, or for reasons unknown. Be it as it may, you all saw what it did to me when I touched it."

A few of the reapers grumble, but Deacon ignores them. "I believe this leaves no choice. Ambrose has to be the Judge."

So much for not wanting to be the center of attention. "No, no I can't be the new Judge." Walking closer to the podium, I lean toward Deacon. "This has to be a mistake," I hiss, eyes darting over the leering crowd. "As Lorcan said, I–I've never exactly had respect for the laws, I don't even want to be in LLAPS. Deacon, we have to find a way for you to take it. Let's go to the Akashic waters. Just you and me—"

"Enough, Ambrose. Don't let anyone hear you," Deacon says, dropping her voice to a whisper. She sighs. "To be honest, it doesn't surprise me much that the scythe chose you."

My eyes widen.

"Think about it. You're a reaper who has lived a human experience. You've seen both ends and rose from the dead, practically. It makes perfect sense."

"Deacon, I believe you will make a far better Judge than I."

"Well, that doesn't matter now, does it? As much as I was ready to take on that scythe," she says, pointing at it in my hands, "I am willing to let the rightful person bear it and follow them just as I did with the Judge. My purpose is to serve the council. I don't care much about power."

I lend her a scornful look. "Deacon, I need to leave and check on Addison. She thinks I died as a human!"

Deacon scoffs.

"You saw her! When I was dying, you got to see what happened, didn't you? Tell me, is she okay?"

"Enough! Ambrose, you need to put her behind you. Addison is fine. She's currently with her brother. Your new role holds a much greater responsibility. The entire council depends on you to return order to LLAPs. You need to pick yourself up and assume your rightful position as Judge." Deacon softens her eyes and sighs. "Look Ambrose, this might be your opportunity to change what you didn't agree with. Make a difference."

Deacon's words resonate with me. What am I to do? The scythe chose me to rule the council. She's right.

Deacon grabs me under my right arm. "Get up here and say something."

I stammer as Deacon steps down from the podium. Every reaper's eyes are fixed on me. I swallow as their icy, cold stares drill into my skull. After a moment, chatter fills the room, sending shivers down my spine. My knees quiver.

"Ahem," Deacon whispers at me.

I blink, shaking off my confusion and ignoring their ear worms. *OK, here goes.* I pick up the gavel, mimicking what Deacon had so readily done before, and bang it on the podium three times. Their talking tapers off.

"Well, is he going to speak?" Lorcan asks.

"Yes, Lorcan. I will speak," I say, shooting him a sardonic glance. The smug reaper sits back, pursing his lips. "Thank you all for your patience. I–I find myself at a loss for what to say. This is all highly unexpected. To be honest," I stammer, "I would prefer it if Deacon were Judge, as she has the most experience, having been our dearest Judge's right hand for so long. Hell, I think Deacon here is the only one who knew his name. We all just called him Judge."

"It was Silas . . ." Deacon says.

A few of the reapers in the back offer a laugh.

"So, what are you going to do to put things right?" Lorcan stands up again. All eyes land back on me, some nodding in agreement.

I look at my new golden scythe. Deacon's words run through my mind again. *This might even be your opportunity to change what you didn't agree with. Make a difference.* I clear my throat.

"I'm going to change a few of the rules about the way we do things."

"Like what? Are you going to allow us to date humans?" Lorcan scoffs, followed with a laugh.

"Now that you mention it, Lorcan, I do intend to change that strict law. You will no longer be persecuted for fraternizing with humans or spending time on Earth. I'm not saying *date humans*. But getting to know humans better will do you all a bit of good. You can all stand to learn a little empathy." Reapers from all corners of the room gasp. Lorcan screws up his face.

"And as for the first order of business. After a quick recess, you will all retrieve your scythes from Deacon and will resume reaping past due deaths on Earth. Millions of people still suffered at the hands of Azazel, and we were not able to do our jobs when their time came. Those spirits need to be directed." My eyes dart around the room. Reapers nod in agreement. My spirits lift. "Azazel has caused enough pain as it is, and we're wasting time talking about it. Secondly, I will need two search teams. One will be for the sole purpose of finding any rogue spirit and bringing them back to LLAPS. The second team will hunt any demons who left the portal and annihilate them."

Deacon coughs and shoots me a look.

"Yes, Deacon?"

"Annihilate them, Ambrose?"

"Correct. Annihilated." I continue. "Next order of business will be to guard the Akashic waters and put guardsmen on alert for anytime a portal opens. We can't take any chances with what could have escaped LLAPS."

"All demons?" Lorcan stands up, a sly smile spreads across his face.

"Ambrose, if I may," Deacon interrupts, "the demons are just creatures from LLAPS . . ."

"Let me repeat myself. Nothing that came out of there was good, and the way to end it is to kill all of them. Any demon with the sense to stay behind will have."

Deacon falls silent and shoots Lorcan an angry look. I quirk a brow at her.

"Deacon, you hate the demons. Why are you so concerned about me killing them off?"

She shakes her head at the crowd, and I scrunch my brows.

"They're LLAP'S creatures, is all. I'd be careful with bending the rules so much. Keep in mind there is an order and a purpose for all things, malignant or not."

"They've caused more damage than good." I raise my voice, turning to the council. "As I said before, I do intend on making changes."

Lorcan leans in on his seat. "Exterminating demons is something I can get behind."

A smile curls up my lips.

ADOPTED HELLPUP

ADDISON

Blood rushes to my face as I stand motionless, staring out from the open window inside my neighbor's house. Her cold, lifeless body lies behind me. She's dead and it's my fault. Minutes ago, Dax and I broke into Mrs. Wilson's house because we heard noises coming from the inside. And from the looks of the Keys right now, a demon had gotten in. But it was too late. The hellhound that followed us from LLAPS and had eaten her spirit is now roaming the neighborhood unsupervised. It's my lucky day, I guess.

I had gone down to hell to save my boyfriend and came back out a demon—and empty-handed. My heart hurts just thinking about Ambrose . . .

I swallow. A part of me hopes Deacon was able to save him. But the cynical side of me knows he's dead. Dax blabbers in the background, and only when he says something about spirits do I tune back in.

"Now there's something else giving orders to collect souls. How many of these demons are doing this bidding, and for what purpose?"

"Hm?" Dax's voice snaps me back to the present. Oh, that's right, I had just finished saying we needed to find Lucifer and convince him to put everything back the way it was, including me. Chasing the devil? Ha. This'll be fun. Especially since he turned me into this, this . . . thing on purpose. Convincing him to help isn't going to be easy, and he doesn't want to be found.

I shift my weight to my other leg. "Let's get out of here." I don't care to stay hanging around my neighbor's house with her body lying here, and we have a hellhound to find.

Dead leaves crunch under my feet as I step out of Mrs. Wilson's house. "Well, now we know some people are in their homes . . . Even if it does mean she was getting her soul sucked out of her."

Dax clears his throat. "Right, but what does that mean for everyone else?" We step out into the street and stare at all the houses. A cool breeze blows past, taking with it brittle leaves and dust. The temperature is dropping. "Feels like winter, or close to it, for Florida at least."

I scrunch my forehead as I take a stride near the house across the street. I left on Valentine's Day. It should be nice and toasty. The twilight from the sun setting casts a shadow on the pavement. "Even with the sun going down. There's no way I could have been gone for that long."

Dax raises an eyebrow as he follows me. "This place is a ghost town. Where the hell is everybody?" Dax chafes his chin. "This worries me."

I squint my eyes toward the end of the road. "Maybe we should take a walk outside of the neighborhood. Might be able to spot the hellhound while we're at it."

Dax wipes his face. "Man, that beast could literally be anywhere."

I lead the way out of the neighborhood. "If only there

was a way to call it, or to cast some light on whatever is out there . . . whatever escaped."

I wrap my cloak around myself. "Is it getting colder?" A gust of wind blows my hood down. The blue skies turn grey and a mist begins to form all around us. The air is so thick I can taste its cold dampness. My body vibrates as it had inside the library. Wait—No, why is this happening? This couldn't have been me—I can't control the weather and I said cast light, not shade!

"What the hell is going on?" Dax says.

I stretch a hand out in front of me. I'm able to see it for a few seconds, and then it vanishes in the growing thickness of the clouds.

"Just great," I say.

"I can't see a damn thing," Dax asks.

"Neither can I. I'm not sure, but stay close."

"Addison, try using your powers to get rid of it."

I concentrate on making the fog dissipate. "Go away," I whisper. The fog splits for a mere second but retracts back at us, thicker than before if that was even possible.

"It's not working!"

"Try again!"

"Dissipate!" The fog darkens to a deeper grey, its smoky swirls moving around us in a circular motion.

"Are your spells acting backward or are they just not working?"

"Thanks! Not helping!" But really . . . What the hell?

"Sh. Stop," he says.

"What?"

He holds out his hand and grabs my arm. "I mean, shut up for a second." Scratching echoes from within the fog. I hold my breath and squint into the thick mist as something moves. *The hellhound? No, it would have whimpered or found us already.*

"Dax . . . There's something there."

Something swooshes in front of us and I take a cautious step back. A black pincer emerges from the fog. My eyes widen.

Ozo? My knees tremble. If Dax didn't have a tight grip on my arm, I may have collapsed. I swallow hard and look again. "That isn't . . ."

The giant pincer slices the air again; this time, seven red eyes glare back at us.

Okay, not Ozo. Actual giant scorpion instead. "Run!"

I nearly trip over my own feet as I pull away from Dax's grip. Scraping sounds ricochet in my ears as its large legs dig into the ground, getting louder and louder behind us. My heart thumps in my chest as I run. There's no time to see where Dax went, but since he's dead, he's faster than me. So I keep running.

A woosh of air hits my back, and the only thing I can think of is the scorpion's giant pincer swinging for me. *Wings would be handy right about now! Or a portal out of here!*

A giant flame lights the road in front of me, but since I'm running so fast, I can't stop myself from crashing into my brother's chest. My eyes move up to meet his. His face is skeletal and caught on fire, as are his hands. Somehow, I don't get burned when I touch him, nor do his clothes catch fire. I pull away and turn around to face the now glowing frame of a giant scorpion.

An image of Azazel using Ozo against me in the mental plane, when I found out he had been pretending to be my friend, Seth, flashes in my memory. Hatred starts to churn the pit of my stomach.

Dax raises one hand over his head and throws a burst of

fire at the scorpion. It hits its exoskeleton but dissipates. He tries again but the blast does nothing. Dax cools off, returning to normal.

The scorpion shakes itself and I take a few steps back until my hands touch the smooth surface of a wall. We're cornered outside of someone's house.

"Addison, do something."

It's my turn. I keep my gaze on the scorpion as I steady my breathing, taking in the thick dampness of the fog. I visualize the scorpion going away. Its pincer rises, poised to strike.

Go away, go away. It's gone, never was. That stupid son of a bitch . . .

The arachnid lets out an ear-splitting wail. Its legs shrivel and shake until they give in to its heavy body. Its pincer becomes limp and the giant body turns itself over, legs curled upward. Its red eyes cry anguish as it stares at me, letting out an anguished cry, making my stomach churn.

Dax's gaze flicks to me. "Shit, alright."

I glance between the scorpion and Dax. "I'm not doing that. Or . . . I'm not meaning to." I stammer. I stop my magick completely. Its legs begin to shake, and its body starts pulsating.

"Can't you stop?"

"I–I don't know how."

"Not that I care about it, but torturing the thing is kind of cruel, Addi—"

"I'm not trying to!"

The cries coming from it start to subside as its heart slows.

"Did you stop?"

I shake my head. "I think it's just dying." My lips quiver.

It gives one last scream as something attaches itself to its pincer.

"Now what?" Dax shouts. Out from the fog, a set of red eyes and snarling teeth jump onto the arachnid. The hellhound grips onto its giant pincer, crunching down on it. After two or three gulps, there's no trace of a giant scorpion ever being there.

The hound licks her lips, walks up to me, and smacks my hand with her tongue. I snap my hand back and clean it on my clothes. "Yuck. Well, at least that put it out of its misery?"

"And look, we found the hellhound."

"She found us." I grip onto its large neck, nudging her to walk. "Maybe we can use her to get back."

"Or she'll lead us to some other giant dwelling creature from hell."

My chest is still heaving. I don't think that screeching sound coming from the scorpion is ever going to leave my brain. "Dax . . . I—"

He pauses and arches a brow, his frown pasted on his face. I know what he's thinking. That I meant to torture that scorpion. I bite down on my cheek. Dax has never looked at me like that before.

"I don't think my magick is working the same way it used to."

"What do you mean?"

"I don't know yet . . . I just feel . . . different. Ever since I transformed into this . . . " I wave down at my body. "A demon . . ."

His eyes search mine, almost quizzically, and I can feel myself getting irritated. "I didn't torture it on purpose, Dax."

"Okay, I know. So you're thinking your magick is different now? I guess that makes sense . . ." He chafes his chin. "You went through a pretty big transformation; I wouldn't expect your magick to stay the same . . . We'll figure this out, but first, let's get inside."

I relax my shoulders and nod. I know I'm different now. I can feel it.

We stride in silence through the mist, weary of anything dangerous and not visible to the naked eye. I grip on tightly to the beast's neck, afraid that if I were to let go a little, she would take it as an invitation to scurry off. Its coat feels soft, just like a normal puppy's coat would feel. Despite it having unsettling red eyes, and rows of sharp teeth, she's actually kind of cute.

The fog swirls before us as we walk down the road. The iron gates of the house become visible and the hellhound starts picking up speed as if excited to be home.

"Not that this'll keep out any giant scorpions or flying hellhounds, but at least there'll be some sort of barrier," Dax reaches over and feels his way to the gates, pulling them in to lock them. He turns to face me. "Wait, can't you put a warding spell around the house?"

"Not a bad idea, but first I need to see what's going on with my magick."

"Fair enough. I know you said you didn't mean to torture it, but I admit for a second there I thought you did."

"No, I–I was focusing on getting it to go away."

Heat smacks us in the face as we step back inside the house. "It's colder out there than it is here. Maybe we should open a window," Dax says.

"And also figure out how to get the electricity running again." I move my hair out of my face and put it in a high ponytail.

"We're not letting her run loose around the house, are we?"

The hellhound pulls free of my grasp, causing me to topple over. I move my arms up to block myself from falling on the wall. "Hey! Come back here!" We run out of the foyer and through the Venetian room, right into the doll room, to find the hellhound cornering a ghostly gnome with sharp claws and teeth. With one gulp, the gnome is food.

"I guess we are, then," Dax says.

The hellhound gleams up at us, wagging her tail and licking her teeth. I search the room for anything else that shouldn't be here. "Coast is clear. I'm starving." I walk out of the room. "Let's talk about what just happened in the kitchen. Come along, Skadi."

"Skadi?"

"Yes, the hellpup."

"When did you name her that?"

"Just now."

The hellhound jumps over us and flies up the stairs. With a pep in both our steps, we follow her, hoping she won't break anything else.

"So why Skadi?"

"Skadi was a Norwegian giant who was also known for being a huntress. She was also called 'The Devourer.' Since our hellhound here has devoured plenty of ghostly creatures and lesser demons, I thought it was fitting."

"Ah."

"It's better than Little Feet!"

Dax smiles back at me. "If you say so."

Up on the second floor, Skadi sniffs around the corners of the house. "Uh . . . Addison, how exactly do these things go to the bathroom? Are they like regular dogs?"

"No idea. But I was thinking . . . Maybe let's not get rid of her just yet. I mean, she did just eat an egregore downstairs."

Dax winces but then nods. "And she devoured a giant

scorpion in just a few gulps. Maybe we can use her to hunt down demons that are out here. And protect us."

"Crowley's gonna be so pissed." A wan smile dances on my lips as I stare at Skadi, who is now chasing her tail and knocking over some fake potted plants that my mother had decorated the house with years ago. I bite down as one of the ceramic pots shatters into small pieces. Skadi sniffs it and starts biting on the fabric flowers.

Like I said, fat chance. "Is it possible to train a hellhound?" The image of Skadi chomping down on Mrs. Wilson's spirit makes its way back into my mind. "Oh Dax, we can't let her eat any of the innocent spirits though!"

"How would we know which ones are innocent?"

"Maybe it's best if we show her not to eat *any* spirit, just to be safe."

"Even the ones who escaped LLAPS? Some of those, probably most, if not all were dangerous criminals."

"That's not entirely true." I remember walking through a tour of LLAPS with Azazel, witnessing lost souls, suicides, some victims of their own self-punishment. The floating heads in that horrible, depressing level. "Maybe some of them need the opportunity to get themselves out of torture."

Dax furrows his brows, posing in his usual brooding posture. "Sounds like we need to discuss what your next moves are."

A low growl comes from the library and my face pales. "Dad!" I jolt up from the couch and slide over to the double doors.

"Don't let her eat dad's spirit if he's back!" Dax yells as he runs up behind me.

"Hey! Get away from him!" What looks like a half-eaten skeletal-face pokes from a shrouded black hood as it looms over my father's body. I raise my hands, hoping to the gods my magick will work this time, when Skadi jumps up and chows down. She starts with the back of its cloak and brings it down to the ground. The demon shrieks, turns, and smacks Skadi across her enormous jaw. Her eyes glow red as she salivates over our tiled floor. The crunching of the demon's bones makes my lip curl upward, but Dax's face twists.

"Ew!"

"Good girl," I say. I turn my attention to my dad and sit by his side as Skadi licks her lips, finishing the demon off.

"Okay," Dax says. "We can keep her." He reluctantly acts like he's about to pat her on the head when she sticks out her giant tongue and licks his hand. "Yuck. Come on!"

"Dax, come here. Dad is really pale and his breathing has slowed . . ."

Creases form on his forehead as he wipes his hand on his pants and nestles to the couch. "Well, he's still alive. That demon must have just been checking him out because there was nothing to eat. He's probably this way because he's been out of his body for too long."

A ball forms in my throat. Come back to us, dad. Where did you go?

Dax scratches at his head. "Why do you think Skadi ate this demon but not the one at Mrs. Wilson's house?"

Climbing back to my feet, I lift the blanket at the end of the couch and cover my dad with it. "I think she probably tried, but that one was more powerful than this one."

"So, she can eat some demons, that's good to know. Shall we get to figuring out your magick situation so we can ward the house?"

I sigh and let my hair down again, rubbing my forehead. "Yes, but first I need to feel some form of normality." I walk to the kitchen and take out the moka and ground coffee.

"How'd you do that back there, by the way?" I ask him.

Dax brings out some crackers from one of the kitchen cabinets for us to munch on. "Do what?"

"You went total ghost rider on me. Your face turned into a skull, and fire surrounded you. Even your hands were aflame. It was terrifying."

"It happened to me before."

"I remember I saw that happening in LLAPS during the battle, and just before we left, but I hadn't gotten the chance to ask you."

"Before that too. The first time was in Peru while I was staying with the Ashaninka."

"The Asha-what?" A chuckle escapes the back of my throat. When was he in Peru?

Dax sighs. "Back when Azazel cast both me and Ambrose out, he took my scythe and dropped me in the Amazon. I was able to stay with this indigenous tribe who looked to me for protection."

My eyes widen and my lips curl into a smile as he goes on.

"One night during an ayahuasca ceremony, their village was raided by another tribe and they killed and hurt some people I got to know. I don't know how it happened, but I physically changed to what you saw back there. If I get enraged enough, I can turn it on."

"That's crazy. So, is this a reaper thing? Could like, Ambrose or Deacon do it if they got pissed off enough?"

"I don't believe so, no. Somehow it's just me. I think maybe it's an undead, and now reaper with powers, sort of thing."

I stick a cracker in my mouth while I wait for the coffee to perk. The kitchen is starting to smell of coffee, and for a moment I can feel like everything is going to be alright. "Well, I think it was pretty kick ass."

"Thanks, I was wondering how it looked. It seems to freak out a lot of people. Didn't do jack to that scorpion though."

"Neither could I. Maybe we just need to develop our new abilities."

Dax nods. "Speaking of abilities . . . what's up with yours?"

Skadi walks into the kitchen, sniffing the floor. I sigh and think about how my arms had vibrated when I had hoped for light. But instead, the exact opposite came. I take out a cracker and give it to Skadi, who licks it right off my hand.

Dax drops his jaw. "Spirits, demons, creatures, crackers. Is there anything this beast won't eat?"

"I think it'll eat just about anything." The moka starts to fill, and I move to get the spoon to make the foam. "My arms vibrated when I said, 'If only I could cast some light on the creatures that escaped earlier.'"

"Okay?"

"And then the fog appeared."

"Well, you said light though."

I shrug. "But that's not the only thing. They vibrated again the same way when I tried to make it go away, and it didn't. And again, when I accidentally started torturing that scorpion."

"So, what are you saying? That you caused the fog? But that's not how your spells have worked in the past. Usually, you think of something and 'so might it be.'" He waves his hand in the air.

"I know, but something's changed. I can feel it." I furiously stir the sugar and coffee mixture in the metal jug until I'm slightly out of breath. "That's not all either."

Dax raises an eyebrow.

The coffee finishes brewing and I pour the rest of it into the metal jug, stirring gently. Skadi has her nose close to the kitchen table right under me. I nudge her away with my knee but she stands her ground. "Earlier, when you were checking the house and I was in the library with dad, I fell asleep for a little bit. I guess I was so shaken up by everything that happened that I dreamt of a replay of what happened in LLAPS.

"Completely normal."

"But then when I woke up, I felt really sad. The room went cold and the mirror on one of the bookshelves cracked from it freezing. My arms vibrated then too."

"So, you caused the mirror to crack, and the fog to appear, and tortured the scorpion."

"Yes, I believe I did." I open up one of the cabinets and take out a small coffee cup and set it down on the table.

"Hey, I'm a reaper now. I can drink coffee too, you know!"

"Oh, sorry. I forgot." I reach over and grab another cup. "Going from undead to reaper has its perks."

He smiles.

"What am I going to do, Dax? What does this all mean?"

Dax takes a sip of coffee and closes his eyes. "Definitely has its perks. Okay, so what do we know?"

I think for a moment. "Lucifer opened a portal and a lot of demons and spirits have escaped, monsters too, evidently."

"Right, and also that there's a higher-level demon collecting souls through minions."

I roll my eyes to the side and take another sip. "I wonder how many minions out here are doing so."

"That's a fair point," Dax says.

"We need to find Lucifer."

"Yes, but I don't think that should be our top priority. It's not like he's just going to turn around, take away your demonic queen thing, or whatever you want to call it, and call all his demons back to LLAPS just because we find him. How are we going to persuade him to do any of that?"

I sigh deeply. Dax is right. What would I even say to him? Can I trap him somehow? This is the freaking devil we're talking about!

"What we need to do is locate any spirit snatching demons and question them so we can figure out how to put a stop to the torment here."

I look up. "Yeah, no, you're right. Setting things back to normal here is the priority. But what about going back for Dad? We can't just leave him there looking for us."

"I agree. But if we go back in now, who knows what could happen and how long we'd be consumed by that place? For now, we're going to have to trust that dad will make it back before his body dies. He knows the consequences better than anyone." Dax twirls the cup in his hand, then sets it down on the table and leans forward. "Can you call him back from here? Or at least put a protection spell on him? Maybe even locate him by opening up a portal directly to him, then I'll go and bring him back."

"Sounds great, but how can I do any of it with my magick on the fritz?"

Dax chafes his chin like he usually does when he's thinking. "We're just going to have to figure out why and how you can control it. What if we have a bit of a trial run?"

I stare at my hands. Skadi sits in front of us with her head tilted sideways, as if trying to understand the conversation. "You mean test out my powers for good and bad?"

Dax shrugs his shoulders. "Might be the only way we

can figure out what's going on with you. Otherwise, we might end up in another evil scorpion situation, and next time it might be worse. Since you seem to have demon magic now, for all we know, the more you use your power, the eviler *you* become."

THE MASTER OF DEATH

AMBROSE

My heavy foot echoes down the hall of the council meeting room as I pace back and forth in front of Deacon as she lays out a few more scythes on a table to inspect them. The other reapers had left to their quarters to wait for further instructions to allow Deacon and I some time to evaluate our plan. Silence has mostly fallen between us since then, the only reason being we're probably in shock. This was meant to be hers, and now I've taken it. Not that I had a choice in the matter, but how am I even to console her? What could I possibly say or offer her to make things better? Despite her telling me earlier that she only cares about serving the council, I know in my bones this is what she wanted. What she's trained for. She has to be gutted.

Each time I turned to face my new golden Judge's scythe on the mantle, I feel a compulsory urge to pick it up. As if it is calling me. The first time I touched it, even though it was to save it from hitting the floor, a bright blue light emanated from it. But that was all. My ability to touch it. And perhaps with all the tension from the courtroom and all of my excitement, I didn't really feel it. Hear it. Sense it. But now, it's almost been a full day, and with each quiet moment, I'm urged to lift it.

And I did. About two hours ago. It's a lot heavier than my other scythe. Or any other reaper scythe for that matter. And taller. At full length, I stand with it leaning against my shoulder if I wanted to, but unlike all the rest, I can make it smaller, keep it as a pocket scythe to fit more comfortably inside my coat or jacket. I turn on my heel and walk to the far end of the courtroom, facing the light stone wall as if reading a manuscript, purposefully ignoring the shimmer of magick that waves across the gold each time I steal a glance at it.

At first, I couldn't put my finger on it. Why was its power so strong? This really is no ordinary reaper scythe. It's old. The oldest, in fact. But what I didn't know or understand was just how much different, and far more superior, it is to every other scythe. The power it wields is unimaginable to any other reaper. I wonder if the Judge had kept that purposefully to himself. If the other reapers knew how much power I now possessed—think they're pissed at me now? And I mean, it's not like I had a choice. I didn't choose for Azazel to turn me human; I certainly didn't choose to die as a human. And how would I have known the scythe would have chosen me for it?

That power though . . . When I touched it last . . . it was like it took hold of me, a lot like electricity—once caught by it, it's hard to pull free. But when I did, it changed something inside me. Every fiber of my being felt alive. Like I could feel more than ever before. Empathy swarmed every inch of me. I heard millions of deaths happening throughout the span of the earth, all happening at once. It was overwhelming. Overbearing. I couldn't handle it and it almost broke me.

But I held it together, and that's why I let it go. I couldn't let Deacon see. For fuck's sake, did the Judge feel like this all the time? He always seemed so . . . calm and collected. Could it be possible that it's different for everyone? The empathic reaper. As if I wasn't a joke already to the other reapers. What the hell am I supposed to do? It's no wonder why the Judge had chosen Deacon as his right hand. He couldn't manage this all alone, no matter how he pretended he could. And she is the perfect reaper to take over. Even I know I'm not responsible enough to be Judge. I'm not into the cause. I'd rather be with Addison.

I dare another glance at the golden scythe and meet eyes with Deacon, a concerned look on her face as her brows are creased. She's watching me pace.

"Something's changed in you, Ambrose. I can usually hear other reaper's thoughts, but I can no longer hear yours."

"Were you ever able to hear the Judge's thoughts?"

"No. His thoughts were always blocked out for some reason . . . Never thought it polite to ask."

I purse my lips and nod. "What am I supposed to do here, Deacon? This was supposed to be your destiny, not mine."

"We don't know our destinies," Deacon says, mimicking me by pursing her lips together. "You're going to do exactly what the Akashic waters intended. You're going to be the new Judge and lead us all out of this."

I throw my arms down. "But why did the Akashic waters choose me? This, I don't understand. "

Deacon folds her arms. "I don't know precisely, but what I said to you before makes sense to me. Perhaps since you became human and were reborn into a reaper you hold a newer and different perspective."

My eyes meet the floor. "I just really want to get to Addison."

"All in due time. But for now, I need you to focus."

"I can do that. At least she has her dagger and can transport herself home."

Deacon winces.

"What is it?"

"Nothing, Addison is fine, trust me. It's just when, after you got stabbed, I shielded you to get you out of there. I caught a glimpse of Addison dropping her dagger right when the ground opened up . . ."

I raise a hand to my temple. "What are you trying to say, Deacon?"

"I'm only hoping Addison does indeed have the dagger."

I lower my voice. "Deacon, putting to rest that she's in danger and is safe, if any demon gets their filthy hands on that dagger, all of LLAPS could fall into a trance under it. Whoever held it would hold the power to rule demons against free will!"

The soft sound of a door shutting splits my attention to the front of the room. "Who's there?"

Deacon walks briskly over and opens the door.

"No need to make a fuss." Lorcan pushes his way in. "I came for my scythe. Do you have it?"

Deacon points to the table. "See if you can find yours."

Lorcan eyes the scythes extended on the table and picks one up. "Good, now I can get busy demon hunting," he says with curled lips. He lowers his eyes over to me as if looking down on me, then flicks his eyes over to the golden scythe on the mantle before making his way out.

Deacon shuts the door.

"Well, that was pleasant," I say.

"Seemed kind of strange to me that he wouldn't just interrupt. He isn't known for being polite."

"He was probably hoping to catch you alone since he hates me," I tell her.

"Yes, well, talk of the dagger would just make him want to hunt demons more, so I'm not worried about him having overheard anything."

I chafe my chin. "I'll set up another search team for the dagger then. Let us hope it hasn't already fallen into the wrong hands."

"Why don't you try practicing by getting rid of this creepy fog?" Dax says as he leans back in his chair in the family room while I stroke Skadi's coat. For the past hour, I've been considering why my change had caused my powers to perform like it was opposite day. I thought becoming a demon would have made me stronger, more powerful. Not the clumsiest with my magick I've ever been. I get up and stretch my arms.

"Should we try doing this outside?" I ask.

"It's up to you, but with the skills you went to LLAPS with, you should be able to do it anywhere, and if you need to use your magick in an emergency later, you'll need to be able to do it on cue. We shouldn't waste any more time. Not to mention—if we go outside now, there might be an emergency, and then you'll screw up."

"Okay, okay . . ." Dax—ever the voice of reason. I rotate my wrists and close my eyes.

"Any minute now."

"Hey! I'm trying to think of what to do." Jeez!

"How about just saying, 'Mist be gone,' or something like that?"

I roll my eyes and face the window, holding my hands in front of me as I peer into the dark fog. Skadi whimpers and scoots up closer to me. Clearing my throat, I say, "Mist be gone!" I lower my arms and pause, but nothing happens. Instead, my arms start to vibrate. I rub them and lean toward the window for a better look. Dax stands and cups his hands around his eyes to see better.

"It's too dark, I can't see anything."

A bolt of lightning lights up the night sky and Skadi howls. I tilt my head back. "Oh, this can't be a good sign."

Dax walks over to a side door leading to the outside patio on the second floor. He unlocks and opens it, sticking his head out.

I cringe as I hear him laugh out loud, followed by the door slamming shut.

"Yeah, you just made it worse," he says.

Oh crap, for real? I run to the door and barge it open. "What do you mean I made it worse?"

I can't even see my hands if I hold them out in front of me. The mist has turned to dark purple and lightning is the only thing that can be seen through the fog. A strong gust of wind hits my chest, pushing me back. I shut the door. "Did I just cause a storm?"

"You may have just caused some sort of *supernatural* storm."

"Great. Why is this happening to me?"

Dax rests his head on his hand. "We'll figure it out. Keep practicing."

"I mean, it has to be because I'm part demon now, right? Or that part in me has been awakened."

"Yeah, maybe you're going through some demonic puberty and your magic is changing."

I scrunch up my lips. "A demonic puberty? Great, just what I needed," I say as I kick an empty wicker basket next to the door. Skadi gets up to start sniffing it, whipping the corner of the couch with her tail.

"Okay, let's start small. Try something else."

"Like what?" I say, throwing myself on the couch.

Dax skims the room. "I'll be right back." He runs out of the family room and comes back after a few minutes holding my poor withered lavender plant. "Here, you're quite the green witch, try bringing this back to life." He places the potted plant on the glass coffee table in front of me. Wonderful, just a reminder of how I abandoned one of my passions.

I hold out my hands and focus on the bright healing energy I know I have in me. Steadying my breathing, as I always do before a spell, I will out the warmth and love I've always felt toward plants, my family, and Ambrose. I visualize the flower springing to life, filling itself with luscious greens and beautiful lavender flowers. My hands warm and I envision my spell working. The warmth at the core of each hand becoming warmer and soothing me as well, a meditation close to my morning coffee routine. Until it starts to feel too warm, and now hot. My nose twitches at the smell of something burning.

"Uhh, Addison?"

I open my eyes and gasp. "I thought I was saving it, I swear!" Before anyone can move to grab some water, the fire goes out and the plant falls to ashes. Wiping the sweat off my forehead, I fall back on the couch. Skadi inches herself to the coffee table to sniff the remains of the plant.

"Skadi, no, don't eat the ashes." Too late, she's already licking the ashes clean.

"I don't think anything can harm a hellhound." Dax says.

"So, what now?"

Dax shrugs and takes a seat, resting his hand on his chin and chafing it.

I squint at the pot. "Hmm . . . I wonder."

"What's that?"

I get up and walk over to the kitchen window to choose another plant. I pick one up that looks like it hasn't been watered and bring it back to the coffee table.

"Trying this again, are we?" Dax says.

"Not quite."

I take a seat and with little to no effort, I mutter the word "burn." Dax jolts up from the chair. His eyes grow big as the plant immediately catches flame.

"Ice," I murmur above a whisper. The plant goes from a blazing flame to cooling down and turning into ice, frost sticking to its stems and leaves. I brush off my hands and sit back.

Dax's lips are parted. Skadi sits next to him, wagging her tail and witnessing the whole thing. I wonder just how much hellhounds understand things.

I break the silence. "Well, I guess that means my powers aren't reversed." My breathing becomes heavy. "They're just evil now."

"No, that can't be true."

"It has to be true, Dax. I'm a demon now. My powers are now demonic. I have demon wings for hell's sake!"

Dax leans forward, his eyes peering into mine. "Addison, look at me."

Arms crossed, I look in his direction but keep my face rigid.

"Addison, you are not evil. Do you understand me?"

I stand up and so does Skadi. "How do you know? I mean, really know? We don't know anything about what's going on with me! Just look outside! Everything I've tried today has turned into something . . . malicious!"

Dax stands calmly and grabs my shoulders. "Addison, all this means is that you have to relearn what you know about using your magick. A demon is only called that because they are from LLAPS, not because they were made of evil. There's no such thing. Only you can decide that."

My chest pounds as I breathe heavily through my nose. I fight to keep my eyes dry as best as I can.

Dax lowers his gaze and lets go of my shoulders. "How's your heart, by the way? I haven't noticed you take your medicine for a while . . ."

"Fine, I think." I rub my chest like I used to, but my heart is steady. "Lucifer said something about me never needing medicine again, so . . . Silver linings."

He quirks a brow. "Huh. That's cool. But I'm serious, Addie. Listen to me, you are not evil, okay? We can figure this all out."

I stay quiet, not fully convinced. My eyes wander off to the side.

"Addison, tell me you understand."

"Yes . . . Okay, fine. Understood."

"So, what do you say, instead of giving up, we go and try to figure out how to get rid of this fog?"

I nod and rub my eyes. "I don't even know where to start."

"Well, I was thinking, what if you cast the fog away as if you were intending it in a bad way?"

I screw up my face. "But how could getting rid of the fog be a bad thing?"

"Like, instead of focusing on positive energy, focus on drawing out anger. But with the intent of getting rid of the fog."

I nod once. "Okay, I think I understand." Turning toward the window, I lean forward once again with my hands held out. I inhale deeply and then take a few breaths, trying to center myself from all doubt that this would work, except normally, I focus on squashing all negative thoughts. And now I have to envision the most horrific occurrence that has happened to me recently.

Here goes nothing. Let's see, which of the many most recent occurrences would summon my deepest rage? It has to be fresh. I press my eyes tightly together as I can see as plain as day Ambrose dying in my arms by the hand of Azazel, the demon who pretended to be my friend. Anger swooshes over me at the remembrance of constantly getting betrayed. Prior to that was my ex-boyfriend, who had been another demonic fabrication. And finally, me turning into the very same thing that had betrayed me before, a demon! I open one eye, but the dark clouds remain the same.

Still? Okay, let's go again.

I squeeze my eyes tighter but this time I don't force any images in my head. This time, the image comes to me.

Of Ambrose. Except, not him. Azazel. My gut wrenches at the sight of Ambrose's facial structure changing, horns protruding from his head, and his naked body, already deep inside me, literally altering to Azazel.

Since it happened, I had tried to suppress it. But here it is. Repeating itself in my mind, no amount of memory wiping spells or alcohol would be enough to take that away.

That did it.

My arms rumble until frost starts appearing on the window.

"Addison? I hate to interrupt, but you're sort of bringing down winter in Florida . . ."

"Let me concentrate!" I spit.

"Just don't want Florida to freeze over. I mean, it was hot, but I hate the snow. Ice? Yuck!"

"Will you shut up!"

A smile creeps on Dax's face.

A red glow emanates from my hands as my arms rumble again. This time, the ice melts, followed by silence outside. The howling of the wind stops. So does the lightning. I drop my arms and look at Dax.

Dax walks over to the door and grabs the doorknob. I give him a nod and he opens it. We're immediately greeted by the South Florida breeze over a hot night. The sea breeze blows through my hair as I peer into the canal, watching the back porch light hitting the terracotta tile. The wind rustles the mangrove leaves, and I can even hear a bird flying through. I take a long sigh and give my brother a hug.

"Sorry, didn't mean to snap."

"Nope, don't apologize. I was doing it on purpose." He looks down at me and smiles.

"I can use a drink. Or two."

Skadi pokes her head through the crack of the door and we both push her inside and shut the door behind us.

"No way, Skadi. You're not going anywhere without us, you big brute."

"She's growing on you," Dax says.

"Yeah well, I've always had a thing for dogs. Just never thought I'd have my very own dog from hell."

Dax chuckles. "Technically not hell. It's more of an inter-dimensional—"

"Shut up, I'm calling it hell from now on."

Dax widens his grin. The fact that he can always be so calm and cheerful during tense situations always made me jealous when he was alive. Now, I appreciate it. "So have you thought about how to train a hellhound?"

I pat Skadi's head as I look down at her. The hellhound looks back up at me with her wide jester grin and large tongue hanging out. "Something tells me she understands more than we think. And I somehow think she'll listen to at least my commands. Maybe not yours though."

Dax scoffs.

Suddenly, a dull pain surfaces in the right lower corner of my stomach and the room starts to sway. I hold my stomach.

"Addison? What's the matter?"

I glance up at him and see two Daxes. Oh, this can't be good. A ravenous hunger forms at the pit of my stomach and I know if I don't get food in me now, I'm going to–to—

"Addie? Talk to me."

I hunch over as the room spins faster. Before I know it, coffee, crackers, and bile rise to my throat, and an uncontrollable urge to keep it in prevents me from making it to the bathroom. I can't stop it. Chunks of vomit spew from my lips, and my chest heaves.

My brother quickly grabs my hair and holds it up as I decorate the clean tile floor with an orangey-brown substance, the vile rancid stench assaulting my nostrils.

Yuck.

When finished, I have involuntary tears rolling down my face. "I'm sorry."

"Don't apologize," Dax says. "What was that about? Are you okay?"

"I am now. Starving though."

After stuffing my face with Oreos and basically any non-perishable I could find in the kitchen, I walk over to the library to check on our dad. My eyes narrow as images of me walking with Azazel form in my mind. I pinch the top of my nose. The way Azazel had me cast my powers while in LLAPS . . . *Didn't I have to find a neutral spot in my mind before casting spells? Maybe there's something to that. But, is giving into this really the best choice? I guess it's the only choice for now.* I turn the light on and press a hand to my father's cheek. Somehow, he seems full of color, and his breathing is back to regular.

"Hey Dax, come here quick!"

Dax bursts into the library, his brows furrowed. "What is it?"

"Look at dad. Doesn't he seem okay to you? His face is fuller and the color is back in his skin. Come, check out his breathing."

Dax puts a hand on his dad's forehead. "He feels alright. What do you think is going on?"

"I don't know, but if you know Crowley, I'm sure he has something to do with it." I smile. My dad would be lost without that clever little owl. "So now what?"

"Now, we rest for the night. Tomorrow, we start hunting demons."

LITTLE WHITE LIE

DAX

I struck a few chords of my guitar by my father's side, to keep my mind occupied while I let Addison sleep. Demon or not, evidently, she still needs her sleep. I find solace in that because it at least means she's still mortal. Half-mortal, maybe, but mortal. Poor thing. This was probably all too much for her. It's easy to lose track of time in the astral plane, but also let's face it, she was in danger out there and she knew it. Put anyone in a dangerous situation over a course of days, where they know they need to keep awake to stay alive, and their minds go into a warrior mode as a defense mechanism to keep them alive. Add in no food, stress, power overuse—if there's such a thing—and then . . . Ambrose dying. It's no wonder she threw up. It would happen to anyone.

For the time being, it's crucial Addison gets her rest.

A whooshing sound comes from behind me.

"I wondered when you'd be coming for me," I say.

"I won't be collecting you this evening, Dax, but I did bring you something." Deacon takes out a scythe as the portal closes behind her.

I put down my guitar and stand up, reaching for my scythe. "Thanks, but I don't feel right leaving Addison alone in all this."

"No, I know. Which is why I'm not here to bring you back. Besides returning all reapers the scythes that Azazel confiscated from them, I've come to give you some news."

"So, I'm not reaping?"

"Not yet at least. I've come to warn you about Addison."

I raise an eyebrow. "Warn me about my sister? What are you talking about?"

"I know about her changes, Dax. We all do. All except one."

My jaw stiffens. "Deacon, she isn't dangerous. What happened to her—we're figuring it out. But she isn't evil."

"Evil is a relative term, Dax. But that's not what I'm here to warn you about. I came to say we have a new Judge, and he–he's put an APB out on all demons, to kill them on sight."

I take a few slow steps toward her. "What exactly does that mean? Who is this new Judge?"

Deacon hesitates at first but then speaks very slowly. "Ambrose is convinced that anything that escaped LLAPS has ill intentions, and in order to rectify all of Azazel's doings, he is releasing revitalizers to come down and collect all and everything, no questions asked."

"Wait . . . That doesn't make any sense. Ambrose is alive? I saw Azazel stab him in the chest—and he was human! And now he's the new Judge?"

Deacon nods. "I took us straight to the Akashic waters. I didn't know if it would work at the time, but it not only closed his wounds, he was restored completely. The Akashic levels also saw him fit to be the new Judge of the veil," she pauses, "even over me." Deacon darts her eyes to the floor.

I stand aghast at Deacon's words. "Why would he put an APB on all demons without helping Addison first? Or seeing that she's safe?"

"That's what I'm doing here, Dax. Ambrose doesn't know about what's happened to Addison. Her case is more serious than just flicking a switch. The more Addison uses her powers, the more dangerous she will become. And there is no reversing it."

"So, reapers are after my sister?"

Deacon nods.

I wipe my face and spin around. "Why not just tell him then?"

"Because, Dax, we need him to concentrate on being a Judge. No distractions. If Ambrose gets wind of Addison being a demon now, it'll ruin everything. He'll be more focused on her than on his new responsibilities. And as far as Addison . . . There's nothing we can do. The Akashic waters won't be able to help her, in fact. She would contaminate it."

"Ruin everything? She's my sister! You don't care because you never cared for her! No, Deacon, I'm sorry—but I cannot keep this from her. If Ambrose is alive, she'd want to know!"

"Really, Dax? Is that even fair? After everything I did to help save her, and this family? After me keeping her and Ambrose a secret from the last Judge all this time?" Deacon's eyes sear into mine without flinching. "The council doesn't think they should be together, and Ambrose is already proving to want to change things. Let's just leave this for after we reclaim the order of LLAPS. Can you at least agree to that?"

My breathing is heavy, but I hold her gaze. "I have to tell her."

"Even if it would mean endangering her?"

My brow arches. "How do you mean?"

"You know your sister better than I do. You should know the moment she finds out about Ambrose she'll jump through a portal and right into Lorcan's clutches. As much as I would want to be there to protect Addison—"

"You best believe I'll be there, and I know Ambrose—"

She interrupts my interruption. "Dax, it would cause a war, and Addison hasn't fully come into her new powers yet. He's after the dagger. Do you want to leave it to chance to see if he'll either kidnap her for it or stick his scythe right through her faster than she can mutter a spell? Or faster than anyone of us can save her from him?"

My lips form a thin line. I don't like this, but she has a point.

"Oh, and Dax? Ambrose intends on cleaning up Earth. Make sure you keep Addison safe, and out of our way."

Deacon's eyes fall over to Orlando's spiritless body.

"What the hell is going on over here?"

"Apparently my father decided to go on a little stroll in LLAPS when he found out Addison was missing."

"And he's still roaming around?"

"Correct. We've been meaning to go find him and bring him back but you know, with all that's happening around town, demons trying to collect spirits and Addison's powers all amok . . ."

"Demons are trying to collect spirits?"

"Yes.."

"Have there been any possessions yet?"

"We didn't walk that far out of the neighborhood, but there is a demon commissioning others to do their bidding by collecting spirits from the living, or newly deceased it seems."

"Well, it looks like I brought your scythe back just in time then. I'll need you here tracking those down."

"Yes, we've already been on that, but Addison is having to learn to reuse her powers."

"Be very careful with that, Dax."

"What will happen?"

"I don't know. But it could be possible that she might permanently become a full demon. An evil incarnate. If she accepts it all, there would be no turning back."

I swallow down hard. "There must be a way to reverse this. I'm still struggling to see the point of why Lucifer wanted her to become a demon."

Deacon shrugs. "You can't reverse it because it was in her blood to begin with. Lucifer just needed a replacement for the queen of the demons, and she fit the profile."

"Right, because of our dad. What about Lilith? Can't she take it over for Addison? What if I find her?"

Deacon laughs. "She's a Queen, but doesn't command the demonic armies, which is what Lucifer intended for Addison to become."

I screw up my face. "Why?"

"Yes, that's what I've been asking myself as well. He has some higher plan, it seems. I do have to get going, Dax."

"Wait, what am I supposed to do with my scythe? If she sees it, she'll know I made contact with you guys and ask about Ambrose. She'll wonder if he's alive, and why he hasn't come to see her. She might even leave again to go find him."

Deacon opens up a portal. "I don't know, be creative. I'll look for your father. I have to go." She jumps in the swirling black portal as I watch her close it behind her. Gripping my scythe, I search for my coat, shoving the staff in the lining.

I'll have to keep this visit a secret for now. At least knowing that my pops will be taken care of puts my mind at ease a little.

45

*T*toss in my covers, shielding my eyes from the light coming in through the curtains. I'm feeling more myself after eating and sleeping a little. I reach for my phone, which should be fully charged by now. Seven fifteen a.m. Seriously? Why am I awake? I sigh as I flip myself around and hug my pillow. Few more hours, please!

But my mind spirals down into a rabbit hole. No idea what that was about last night. I don't normally throw up, so it can't be from stress. I mean, yes, I did throw up while in LLAPS, but I mean . . . I had just found out the most horrible disgusting thing ever. But now? Magick overuse maybe?

Kicking off my duvet, I open my eyes slightly and gasp, propping up in bed. I inspect the necklace Ambrose had given me. If it glows, it means he's nearby. *Is it . . . ?* But no. When I look down, it's not glowing. *Did I dream it?* Maybe it was just sunlight reflecting off the pendant. I roll my eyes. Best to not get my hopes up. The soft glow of sunlight coming through my mauve drapes sends shivers down my spine. For a second, I think I'm still in the astral planes and my stomach roils. The tight pain returns, near the bottom right of my pelvic region. I feel a little dizzy but not as bad as yesterday.

Changing these curtains will be the first thing on my to-do list when this is all over.

Fuck it. Can't sleep and too much to do. I yawn and get up out of bed, picking up the sheets I kicked to the floor.

Dax is already in the kitchen with coffee waiting for me on the stove. "Sleep well?"

"The strangest thing happened," I say while pouring myself a cup. "I thought I saw my necklace glow. You know, the one Ambrose gave to me."

"You thought it did?"

"Yeah, but I could have been dreaming."

Skadi whimpers from underneath the table.

"What's wrong, girl?" I crouch down to see under the table, and to my surprise, the hellhound is shivering.

Dax raises an eyebrow. "A whimpering and shivering hellhound? That's not a good sign."

I bend my knees slightly to meet Skadi's face, which is practically hitting the top of the table. "Hey girl, what's this all about? Are you hungry? We're going to go find you some yummy egregore or nasty entity to eat today." Skadi howls in complaint, gets up, and starts pacing. Then she lies back down near me as if not knowing what to do with herself. I straighten up and scratch Skadi on her head.

"Think maybe she's hungry."

"Or bored," Dax says. "She hasn't found anything to torment in nearly twelve hours."

A loud roaring sound comes from outside, and Skadi runs and hides under the dining room table. We both raise our brows and look at each other.

"Oh boy, here we go." I move the sheer kitchen balcony curtains over to the side and peer out. "What now?"

"Cast any spells this morning, sister?"

"Please, I haven't even had my coffee yet."

"Well, let's go take a look then," Dax says as he runs for the stairs. I follow close behind.

"Dax, look at Skadi," I say as I get a glimpse of Skadi hiding under the table and away from the windows. I expected her to follow me.

"The fact that a hellhound who seems dumb enough to eat everything in sight and meant to hunt things down is actually shivering and afraid under a table is really unnerving," he says as he reaches the top of the stairs.

"Whatever is happening must be bad, and this time it definitely is not because of me!"

On the terrace, we stare up at the sky as clouds form together as a never-ending sheet of dark purple. Holy fuck. A sharp lightning bolt strikes loud enough to make me drop onto the tiled rooftop and cover my ears.

"It sounds like a train wreck!" I gape up at Dax, but he's staring at the sky . . . *He probably can't even hear me!* Even if I'm able to concentrate through this racket to make it stop, where do I even start? It's hard to concentrate through the deafening thunder.

Then suddenly, it stops.

We glance at each other, suspecting something is about to happen. I slowly climb to my feet and rub my ears. I turn toward my brother and shrug.

"Is it over?" I ask. Dax slowly shakes his head, unsure of a response.

Then it happens.

Portals open up from all directions, in the sky, out in front of us, behind us, and above the ocean. We back up into each other. Something tells me we need to book it to the house but neither of us makes a move. The portals remain open for minutes, without anything coming out.

"What's happening?" I yell.

"Don't know, something's coming out."

"Something? More like a shit ton of somethings!"

Dax stays quiet. My heart skips, remembering my necklace. I glance down and take it in my hand. *It isn't glowing now though. Could it be broken somehow?*

What else could frighten a hellhound but hundreds of reapers coming down? Maybe Ambrose is alive after all and on his way down? Maybe they're all coming down to stop all these demons and put them back! I drop my shoulders a bit and relax my jaw, realizing I had been clenching it. I spin around slowly. *What are they waiting for?*

"Maybe this is a good thing," I say.

Dax shoots me a cold stare. "How do you figure?"

Low hissing sounds come from afar, followed by a loud whistling as dark shadows start to drop down the portals like bombs.

My mouth falls open. "I just thought that maybe those would be reapers coming through."

Dax grabs my arm, pushing me behind him. "Reapers don't usually make this kind of a grand entrance."

He's got a point. The whistling grows longer and louder as more dark figures fall from portals closer to us.

My eyes widen as I recognize the deep blackness that goes on forever, like a black hole in space. Already the darkest emotions from the corners of my mind are beginning to rise to the surface, interrupting my concentration on the task. And what task was that? Close all the portals? Yeah right.

Remembering my first interaction with the revitalizers

in LLAPS, I block my mind with a bright shade of white and blank my brain for a few moments. I muster the strength to move.

"Dax, we gotta go!"

"They're revitalizers!" Dax calls out over the whistling. "They're being dropped on us from LLAPS!

"Yes, I know!"

"We need to shield the house from them! Come on!" We fly down the spiral iron staircase in two jumps and barge back in through the French double doors, slamming them shut. Skadi howls on the second floor, following us with her eyes as we run down the steps.

I slide into the library and dart to the shelves, picking up our father's grimoires to skim them for answers. Anything that can help us ward ourselves against these things.

Usually, warding against people, I can do. But revitalizers? They haven't exactly been on my radar over here.

"It would really help if he was here to tell us which book to use!" Dax says.

"I'm not even sure there is one." I take a breath. "No; we can do this. It'll be in one of his books of shadows. He's been working on astral projection sigils for ages. He might have one in here." I crouch down, opening one of the cabinets where my father keeps his writings, and start pulling them out, one by one. Dax joins me.

"Sigils for protection during astral travel . . . hope he took that one with him," I mutter.

"Hurry!" Dax says as he flips through the pages of a green leather-bound book with no title. I pick up a massive tome off the floor, bringing it onto my lap. I swipe away the dusty film and read the title: *Dragons of Sidhe.*

"Huh. Don't think what we need will be in here," I say, pushing it back onto the floor. "I don't see anything in here that will work. How long do you think until they start raiding people's houses?" I ask.

"Wait, there's more in the back." Dax reaches over and pulls out a brown leather-bound book, tied by a leather rope. He unravels it and wipes off the dust. "This one's old. Do you think something here will be useful?"

"It doesn't hurt." I take the book from him and open it. "He used to astral project a lot when he was younger and sigils were always his thing, so maybe." I open it to the table of contents and skim down the list.

"Found it."

Dax's eyes light up. "Seriously?"

"It says here: 'Wardings Against Astral Beings on Earth.'"

"Excellent, what do you have to do?"

I flip to the page and try to decipher my father's handwriting. "Some of this scribble has been faded over the years. Remind me to digitize all this after this is over."

"Come on, Addie. There's no time."

I keep skimming the page. "OK, you're going to have to help me with this. Go through every wall facing outward, and every window, and draw this symbol, repeating these words: *tueri contra mortem.*"

"Protect against death?"

"Best to keep it general. We don't have a word for revitalizers."

"Got it, but what about my special will and all that? I don't practice magick, Addison. You and dad do."

"Dax, from what I've seen you do, you have more *will* than any of us. Go do it; I only have you!"

Dax sighs as he stares at the sigil.

"Take the book with you, I have it memorized. Start at the third floor since it's a vantage point. I'll take the first floor. We'll meet back on the second floor to finish it off. And be careful. You're my only hope."

Dax chuckles. "Okay, got it."

"Dax, may the force be with you."

"Alright Addison, I get the reference. Meet back here."

"It's a plan."

Skadi growls outside of the library with intervals of cries. "It's gonna be okay Skadi, we got this!"

I dash down the stairs and start in the bar area since the room has large glass windows, easy to see through. I focus on my will and draw a large mental picture of the sigil in my dad's book, then repeat the words. "*Tueri contra mortem.*"

The doors fling open, letting in gusts of wind. "Shit! I forgot about my magick being different." I rush over and shut the doors, locking them. Skadi is barking wildly behind me.

"Shush Skadi, let me think!" *How do I do this?* I grab on to my hair and pull. Okay, yesterday, I made the mist go away by concentrating on my hate instead of tapping into my happy energy. I close my eyes and concentrate on how much I hate Azazel again. This time, when I open them, the sigil I crafted in my mind is floating visibly in the air as if on fire, just like the symbols floated in LLAPS. I turn around to finish the rest of the house, with Skadi following close behind.

As I focus on the front door, a dark mass eclipses the chandelier. I take a step back, shielding Skadi from exposure. The revitalizer looms toward me, growing in size. Its hollow void expands, readying itself to swallow me and anything else that lives. My ankles freeze in place. I try to lift my feet, but I can't move. It has me in its trap. I close my eyes to picture just a color, any color, white, beige, green. Skadi grips my jeans with her teeth, trying to pull me away, but is tearing at the fabric instead. Good girl, Skadi. At least I know she won't desert me.

My breathing hollows. None of my attempts are working, it's too late. It probably got in when I messed up the spell at the bar. A dizzying weight presses down on my head, making everything go black. I hear a loud growl and then a swoosh of air passes me by. And then the hellhound cries.

I land on the floor with a heavy thud. The last thing I see is the deafening void of darkness about to devour my soul. And a bright blue light.

GUARDSMAN AT THE DOOR

ADDISON

"**A**ddison? Addison! Are you alright?"

Dax's booming voice makes me wince as the house comes into focus. Skadi licks my right cheek and ear as I sit up on the floor and rub my throbbing head.

"Are you alright? You hit your head hard."

"Yeah, I think so. I have a headache. What happened?"

"I heard you yell, so I came down as fast as I could. If it wasn't for Skadi here, the revitalizer would have gotten you."

I pat Skadi on her head and climb to my knees. "I thought I saw—" Slow is good. The room is starting to spin, and I don't want a repeat of last night.

"Saw what?"

"A blue light, like, from a scythe. Did you see anyone here?" But it couldn't have been Ambrose. That's impossible. And if he were still alive, if Deacon had somehow saved his life, he would have come for me already. I fight to press down the idea that he had come to save me.

Dax shakes his head. "No Addison, I'm sorry. No one else other than you and Skadi was here when I came down."

"Hm, it must have been in my mind then. You see visions when those things are over you sometimes."

"Yeah, probably." Dax shifts awkwardly in place. "We should get you some water."

The pounding in my head gets worse as I try to fully stand this time. I let myself fall back down with only my elbows holding me up. The floor is good. The couches seem too far away from me despite them being in the same room. Dizziness sweeps over me. "What about the wardings?"

"I finished them all. The house is safe."

My brow twitches. "You placed them all by yourself?"

"Well, all except the ones you did."

I fall silent, pursing my lips.

Dax smiles smugly. "You're not impressed? You can check them if you like."

"No, I believe you. Just, how long was I out for? That was a three-person job and there were only the two of us. You sure you didn't see a blue light?"

Dax shakes his head. "No blue light, Addie."

"Right, OK, sorry. Well damn! Good job you! See? I knew you could do it!"

A sheepish grin appears on his face as he passes his hand through his black hair. "Yeah, you were right. Guess I'm stronger than I thought."

Banging on the door makes me jolt upward, my stomach aching as I get up too quick, forcing myself to my feet. Skadi growls and digs her paws into the floor. I hold my brother back as he aims to peer through the window on the other side of the staircase.

"Be careful."

"Don't worry." He ducks his head under the stairs and cups his hands together to see out into the dark of day. "It's a guardsman."

"No freaking way! The ones with no eyes, and axes?"

"Yep, that'd be the one."

"What the hell is it doing here?"

"Probably checking every house. It looks like LLAPS has released its guards and cleaners down to Earth to try and fix this mess."

I tilt my head back and look down to the side, flicking my gaze up at him. "Could this potentially be a good thing?"

"What do you mean?"

"I mean, who sent them? Who's in charge of LLAPS?"

"Depends who you ask, I guess. But mainly the reapers make these kinds of decisions."

"Well, this is a largely bold decision. I mean, revitalizers? They eat everything. Transporting them who knows where. At least the guardsmen, once they take off their heads, send them back reanimated. Right?"

Dax squints his eyes. "Who told you that?"

"Dea—Oh, I guess Azazel did." I remember how Azazel had disguised one of his minions to look and act like Deacon the entire time I was in LLAPS, under the false pretense she was there to save Ambrose.

"Right, well the revitalizers relocate energy in a way that breaks it apart and releases it out into the universe, to be consumed in different ways. Or it takes on another form. The guardsmen definitely do what you said, almost like a game to the escapees. But I'm not sure what happens to them out here. Or us for that matter."

"So, this brings me back to . . . Why would the reapers do this? If they did, I'd assume they know what they're doing, and it'll be a good thing. But this doesn't seem good. And I feel like at least Deacon would have warned us by now. But no word from her, or any of the reapers."

Dax quietly steps away from the window and walks over to the bar to get me some water.

"And somehow I'm the one meant to control the demons? That's what really gets me. How exactly am I supposed to do that? I'm not even comfortable with these new powers yet. I hardly understand them." I follow Dax into the bar and plop onto a tall chair facing the counter.

"Do hellhounds drink water?" He asks.

"No idea. You can try, I guess." I watch him pull a bowl out of the bottom cabinet of the bar and open the sink faucet to fill it. "Could demons be behind the opening of these portals? Like, higher-level ones?"

Dax shakes his head and shrugs.

"Do you have any ideas?"

Dax raises an eyebrow. "Not really, no. I do know that these revitalizers will take even the good spirits though. I don't think any demon worth their weight would be phased by any of them. They're used to them hanging around LLAPS. They must have some sort of protection or shield we're unaware of."

"Didn't you learn of any of that during your mentorship with Ambrose?"

Dax lets out a chuckle. "No, Ambrose was always set on the task, and never really meddled or discussed demon affairs."

"Ambrose? Not meddle?" Ha. I arch a brow.

"No, seriously. He only meddled with us because Azazel causing me to die to manipulate you was a meddle in itself. He was meddling to stop the meddling." Dax crosses his arms.

"I see. So, what should I do?" Since I'm the one supposedly tasked with controlling demons.

He leans forward on the bar. "You mean, what should we do?"

I take a sip of the water Dax had placed in front of me and swoosh it in my mouth. The cold fluid from the tap makes me feel more alive and awake as it soothes the lining down my throat. "Actually, I was thinking that maybe with the revitalizers out there, dad could be in trouble with the ones in LLAPS, and it also might be risky with him coming back. I think we should split up. I can take care of this on my own, I'll have Skadi with me. You should go find him."

"First of all, no. I'm not leaving you to handle this on your own. Secondly, if dad's spirit comes back to his body, he'll be under the wardings of the house. And thirdly, I am sure Deacon is already aware of dad being there. She probably just has enough on her plate, so she hasn't come, but I'm confident that she won't let anything bad happen to him."

My forehead wrinkles. He does have a point. The reapers would become aware of there being a human spirit haunting their corridors. But more so, Deacon would have caught wind first, since she would recognize him. At least I'd imagine so. But even still. "How can you be sure she knows?"

"Because Deacon likes to know everything and is always hanging around the Akashic waters. Relax; Dad is fine. And I'm staying here with you."

I scowl, but Dax gives me a pressing nod. Something about leaving my dad out there without knowing for sure he's okay ties my stomach into knots. Dax seems sure though. And I don't want to be alone right now, especially feeling this queasy with so much to do. "Fine. So, the first thing we need to do is hunt down demons and question them. If any of them give us trouble then, well"—my eyes move down to Skadi, who had ignored the water bowl and was licking her foot—"Skadi will have a meal to eat."

Dax curves his lips and nods.

"As for the spirits who escaped, and any on Earth that are in danger"—I flick my eyes from side to side—"we'll have to round them up somehow."

"Ha, and take them where? You know how many spirits we're talking about?"

I purse my lips together. I know he's right, but I'm scrambling for a plan here.

"Could be billions! Take them where? Here?"

I shrug. "Do you have any better ideas?"

"Um, hello? Do you *want* poltergeists? Because *that's* how you get poltergeists!"

I chuckle.

"In this house, forever!" he chides.

"Especially all of LLAPS's finest incarcerated," I add. "But we can't just let them get eaten. Dax, they deserve a chance at redemption."

"Boy, Azazel really did a number on you, didn't he?"

I sigh. "I admit he did get his point across with me about some things."

"Well, I hope not about all things. As for any spirits who were already here on Earth, if you care about those, this will be tricky. Spirits with unfinished business won't want to go but are in danger from the revitalizers. Reapers should be around soon anyway to collect any of the dying or recently deceased."

My head jerks up. "Without a Judge? How do you know this?"

"Well—I, uh, know that the Akashic waters would choose a new one in the off chance that the old Judge stepped down or—" He lets his sentence linger.

My elbows drop off the bar. "It's probably Deacon."

"Yeah, probably."

"She probably would be cold enough to just hit reboot and get rid of everything."

Dax clears his throat. "Well, my fierce leader, now that you've devised a plan, how are we going to execute it?"

"I'm going to do what I always do when I need to figure stuff out. I'm going to check dad's library for help."

Without electricity, the library is dark. Dax finds a bright lantern we keep in the hurricane closet for emergencies and sets it on the coffee table at the center of the library. I also light a few candles on the bookshelves, to help light up the words a bit.

"So much for missing the Florida sun. It's like we're back in LLAPS with whatever is going on making it so dark."

"What exactly are we looking for in here?" Dax says as he finishes putting back all of our dad's books of shadows that he's written during a lifetime of sorcery while looking through each one slowly.

"I doubt anything would be in there. My guess is to check books on druids or shamans. Anything to do with crossing between worlds, which is what we need to do with these spirits. I just need to find an efficient way of doing it."

Dax puts back the last book of shadows and closes up the cabinet, stretching his legs as he gets up to find what I'm talking about.

I pass my fingers through a dusty collection of old books until I reach one with green leather binding. "Aha, I think I found it."

"Already?"

"Well, it isn't from a published book, *per se*. It's a copy from one of dad's old colleagues. A druid who taught dad the use of a magickal crane bag. I had an inkling it would be here, so this is what I was after." I hold the green leather-bound book down to the lantern to better make out the lettering. "I really need to digitize all of these one day."

"So, what's it say?"

"The good news is a spirit can be carried inside of a crane bag just like it can other magickal objects. And since spirits are weightless, it can hold an infinite number of them."

Dax screws up his face. "So, they'd be jumbled in there altogether, all on top of each other?"

"Not exactly. The crane bag's magick makes it much larger on the inside than it looks on the outside."

I refrain from rolling my eyes the moment I look up to see a goofy wide grin on his face. "So, like a TARDIS?" he says.

"I guess, yes."

Dax sighs. "So, what's the bad news?"

I close the book. "The bad news is I took dad's crane bag with me to the LLAPS so I could take my medicine with me."

Dax runs a hand through his hair. "So, what do we do? Isn't there a spell you could use to summon a lost object?"

My eyes light up. "Dax, you're a genius!" I drop the book on the couch and make a dash to my bedroom.

"I know. Are you coming back, or should I follow you?"

Ignoring him, I rummage through my top drawer and bring out a brown, wooden-bound book this time with a shiny gold Celtic knot on the cover.

"I'm always losing my car keys, so dad gave me this

book," I say, flipping the pages. "I probably don't even need to look at it because I've done it a dozen times already."

"Right, but will it bring something back from LLAPS? Seems kind of far away, as opposed to you summoning your keys from somewhere in the house."

"Only one way to find out."

"Wait, Addison." His features are pensive in the flickering lights of the candles.

"Keep in mind your magick is different now. We don't need the opposite happening."

"Shit, I keep forgetting, thanks. Damnit, this changes the spell." I close my eyes. This time instead of summoning a memory, I intend to conjure up fierce rage from the pit of my gut. I already know what it feels like and how to get it. The process of finding it through memory is now a thing of the past for me. I hold out my hands and picture the object clearly in my third eye. My hands warm, and then become increasingly hotter by the second. Once I feel the magnetic pull of energy from hand to hand, I begin to fill it with the colors of the crane bag, the shape, and imagery, including its black leather form and feathers that cover it. I visualize the drawstrings attached to the ridge while maintaining my dark rage.

The energy between my hands starts to feel firm, like mass materializing from the ether—because ultimately that is what I'm doing—summoning physical matter, careful not to misplace it. Once the smell of leather surfaces itself into my nose, the senses needed to complete the spell for the summoning of a magickal object is complete. The rest of it is easy. I can smell it, feel it. A little bit more energy and my will is done.

My rage eases away, replaced with excitement, and a touch of arrogance, I'll admit—but I don't care. I open my eyes to see not only the crane bag in my hands but what's inside of it. I drop my jaw and take out the dagger.

"Holy shit," Dax says.

"Dax, my dagger! What was it doing inside my crane bag this whole time?"

"Looks like you summoned more than you needed."

"No, this is great! I can use this!"

"Addison?"

"What?" I stop and turn as Dax looks around the room. The windows of the library are covered in frost.

"You said that the last time this happened, you were sad?"

"Mhmm."

"And when you were trying to revive the plant, you were upset. So, it caught fire?"

"Yes."

"Okay, so you burn things when you're angry, and freeze them when you're depressed."

"I really don't know."

"What were you thinking of just now while doing the spell?"

"Nothing, I summoned the same feelings I felt from before. I didn't have to think of a memory this time, I didn't want to be brought back. I was afraid of calling any attention to the house with those things outside."

"So, you summoned rage on its own?"

"Yeah."

"I don't think that's good, Addison."

"It felt like the right thing to do, and it takes forever to go through memories. It's like I passed that stage now or something."

Dax lets out a brooding breath.

"We'll figure it out after all this is over. For now, I just need to get the job done. Besides, it's only frost. I didn't freeze the room. It was boiling in here earlier anyway."

"Well, it looks like you're dealing with the elements. Be careful."

"I will." I attach the dagger to my side and tie the crane bag to my belt loop. "Let's go."

Outside, Skadi whimpers by my legs. "Don't worry, Skadi, I promise I won't let them get you."

The Florida air isn't coated with its regular heat, and the sky isn't blue. Dark, purple clouds blanket the once-blue sky of the Florida Keys.

ADDISON

We step out into the moonless night of the neighborhood. Skadi shows her teeth as I lock the gate behind her, not that it needs it with all the warding we—Dax—put on the house. The hellhound moves slowly out in front of us, her head low and ready to attack anything she can't eat. Dax and I both arch our heads and look up at the sky. Revitalizers have circled the house, probably waiting for us to come out.

"Don't move," Dax says.

Skadi opens her mouth and lets out a deep, menacing growl.

"What do we do?"

"Just back away very slowly, out into the street."

"Won't they notice us walking?"

"Not if you keep a clear head and move slow." With our backs touching, taking one step at a time, and making sure none of the revitalizers spot us, we make our move slowly into the street. Once outside the entrance gate, we pick up speed to clear the distance.

Tavernier Key is reminiscent of LLAPS with its dark

purple sky, and demons and guardsmen roaming around. I wrap my coat around me; another strange happening is the fact South Florida is becoming a bone-chilling cold in its new environment.

Standing in one of our neighbor's yards, I turn toward our house and scan the front yard entrance, taking in the new atmosphere. "How much of LLAPS is seeping in?"

"And how far does it go?" Dax is wearing his usual reaper uniform with a scythe emblem on his right collar flap.

"Beats me," I mutter under my breath.

"At least there's no mist now."

"Yeah, just an eerie purple darkness with the occasional black hole."

Dax sighs. "Alright, Skadi. We're following you. Go find some demons."

"Or spirits," I say.

"Should we knock on people's houses? To check if they're inside, stunned and at the mercy of some demon?"

"They probably won't answer, but I can kick the door in again."

"Yeah I mean, where is everybody?" The neighborhood is still a ghost town. Probably for the best. If people aren't awake to see what's happening, that should make things easier for us, right? The last thing we need is a scared mob of people.

"Maybe we should walk a bit further to check on the main street. We didn't last time because of the neighbor." Cautious of making any noise, we creep down the road. Despite the lucid darkness, it's easier to see without the mist. The air, cold and dry but unmoving. We pass the statue of a manatee holding a mailbox under a gumbo limbo tree, not one leaf moving under the stillness of the wind.

I think I hear a soft rumbling coming from beside me. I snap my head toward Dax, who shifts uncomfortably, tugging on his coat.

"What was that?"

"Hm? Oh, no idea."

Skadi growls and barks before taking off at full speed. I jump at the hellhound's sudden move and take off after her. Dax follows close behind while I jump over some lifted roots on the sidewalk to keep up with a flying hellhound.

"Skadi, what is it?" I call.

Skadi, determined and on the hunt to grab and potentially eat whatever she sees, flies over a fence. "Shit!"

"Now what?"

"Now, give me a boost." Dax helps me up and I jump to the other side, toppling over a little when I land. Dax lands swiftly beside me after easily jumping over it in one cool motion. I catch a glimpse of a translucent spirit floating to the other side of the yard, which leads to the street.

"Skadi, no!" I pick up speed but then stop.

Skadi chomps her mouth shut but misses it by an inch and the spirit is gone. I jog past someone's swimming pool to reach Skadi when the hellhound easily jumps over the next wooden fence.

"Training this beast is gonna be a bitch," he says.

"Come on."

We jump over the fence and climb down to the sidewalk next to the road. Skadi is up on a tree and quickly jumps down when she sees us. She licks her large teeth and wags her giant whip of a tail.

"Oh, Skadi, no. You can't eat those." I hunch over and scratch the hellhound behind the ears.

"Addison? Look up."

I stand up, furrowing my eyebrows at Dax, who is gazing up at the sky. The further out I see, the bluer the sky is. The purple sheet of clouds seems to merge with the clear blue sky of the day just outside of the neighborhood.

"What does this mean?" I say, taking a few steps toward the main road.

Dax chafes his cheek.

"Is it emerging, covering the rest of the world slowly?"

Dax shakes his head. "Possibly. Maybe they're isolating in segments. Or just anywhere there's demonic activity."

"That would make sense, but I still don't see any cars out."

"We should keep going."

"Spirits are going to be more translucent in broad daylight. How will we see them? Do you think Skadi can?" Dirt kicks off the ground as Skadi takes off in another sprint.

"That answers that question!" We cross the street, chasing after her. I can't see what she's hunting, but I take off after her. I don't want another spirit to get away or get eaten.

I stop right at the foot of the steps of an independent bookstore. "Where did she go? Do you see her?" No sign of the hellhound or any spirit nearby.

"Maybe using a hellhound to hunt wasn't such a good idea," Dax chimes in.

I cup my hands on the glass window of the bookstore and peer inside. I wait a few moments to see if I can spot any sudden movements from inside. Where did she run off to? The bookstore is normally empty, so it being deserted is nothing new. It's usually only open on weekends and holidays, so my parents always assumed it was a money laundering business. I've never seen anyone actually shop here.

The store is small. Three bookcases placed against the walls, with a few books stand in the center. Not a soul in sight. Not even Skadi.

"Addison, come look."

I walk over to where Dax is looking through another window. I press myself against it and see someone standing there, presumably the cashier from the looks of it.

"Woah, I never even knew anyone came here."

"Well, someone certainly works here."

"Why are all the lights off then?"

"Addison, look at the cashier. What's different about her?"

I study her. The lady has blonde, shoulder-length hair and is wearing a lavender T-shirt, with a long-checkered skirt. She's looking down at the desk by the cash register.

"I don't get it, what's wrong with her?"

"She hasn't moved a muscle since we got here."

I raise my eyebrows, widening my eyes. "You don't think?"

"Let's check." Dax tries pulling the door handle, but it's locked.

"Right, why would a bookstore that's presumably open, with a cashier working, be locked?" Dax looks around for something.

"What are you doing?"

Dax grabs a big rock from a nearby tree. "Stand back."

"Oh, shit." I run behind Dax and grab my head as he flings the rock hard, into the glass window. The glass shatters all over the floor. I scan the area to see if anyone else is around. But how would there be?

Dax enters the bookstore, the glass crunching beneath his boots. I try stepping over it as best I can.

"Hey, you there," Dax calls out to the cashier who hasn't

budged a smidge, despite the breakage. He starts to walk toward her, slow enough not to alert anything potentially lurking nearby.

Skadi comes out from behind the counter and growls viciously at Dax, causing him to pause.

"Skadi, no! What are you doing? Come here, girl!" I call to her.

The hellhound shows her teeth and crawls toward Dax, digging her claws into the blue carpet.

"Uh, Addison? Why is your hound turning on me?"

Laughter comes from the other end of the store. A woman's deep voice emerges from the shadows. "You can't control a hellhound, especially when you come between them and their food."

"Who are you?" I spin around but don't see anyone immediately in the vicinity.

Dax flicks his fist, causing it to catch on fire. "Show yourself!" he demands. He's getting good at that.

The sky outside grows as dark as it is nearer to the house. It must be encompassing the rest of the Keys at a fast rate. The store lights flicker until they shut off again.

The cashier's neck creaks as she looks dead at us, her eyes a pure white, hiding her pupils behind a thin film.

Tiny hairs at the back arms prickle as I struggle, for the first time since LLAPS, to keep my fear at bay. *Whatever comes your way, Addison, you got this. You've been through it before.* The cashier opens her mouth and lets out a loud and long wail, weakening my knees.

"What's wrong with her?"

"Nothing, only that I'm wrenching her soul from inside her dying corpse," the voice says.

"Where are you? Show yourself!"

Skadi whips her tail, tossing a stack of books on the

floor, and leaps on the counter. I make a dash for the hell-hound, readying my crane bag in my hand.

A shadowy figure emerges from a hidden corner of the store. "Enough. This spirit is mine for the taking." A tall woman with long, black, luscious curls and full red lips, wearing a flowy black dress, releases a spirit out of a similar pouch to my dad's crane bag. A deep sadness emanates from it as if she'd dropped a bomb purposed to fuel all of my hidden worries and depression, yet I can't take my eyes off her. She walks with celestial determination. As if she owns any ground she walks on. And when she looks straight at me, I notice her eyes are pure black. Demon. And here with one purpose. To kill and take souls. Not on my watch, bitch.

I drop my gaze at an opaque little ball of energy morphing itself into a floating mushroom. Easily distracted, Skadi turns her attention from the cashier and with one leap toward the ghostly fungus, swallows it whole. The woman releases a few more, some looking like mushrooms, others looking like trees and rocks. With each opaque object the woman drops, different emotions soar from them; some angry, some fearful, others sad.

"Egregores?" I can't believe how easy it is to feed the hellhound, or to have her distracted.

"You do have a lot to learn, young demoness."

"Who are you?" My stomach quivers at her calling me a demon.

"I am Rezmelda, demoness of foul emotion."

"What do you want with this lady?"

"Oh, it isn't what I want, but just the way it is right now." Rezmelda pulls her long hair away from her face and casually walks over to the cashier.

"Someone sent you. Who?" My hand moves over to my dagger hanging from my belt loop.

"So many questions. What you should be asking is how to make egregore treats to keep your pup in line. Or how do you harness more of your power? But all I hear is, 'Please don't take that poor woman.' My dear, don't you see there's a new order at play here? Life on Earth matters not anymore."

I unloop my dagger and point it at Rezmelda. "Answer the question: who sent you?"

Rezmelda begins to laugh. Her eyes fall on the dagger and fix on it as she walks. The skin of her hand turns from a pale skin color to a shade of rotting flesh, brown and then black, with shriveled skin, reaching halfway up her elbow. Her fingernails grow long and claw-like. She raises one eyebrow, still staring at me with her deep red lips. She closes her claws around the cashier's neck.

"No, stop it! Leave her alone!"

The cashier's body trembles and the girl falls to her knees. Her lips part and a light blue spirit emerges from her mouth.

Dax steps forward next to my side. "Enough!"

"You don't command me, reaper!" She hisses.

"There are plenty of other spirits roaming around, of people dying whose spirits are there for the taking. Why kill an innocent?" he says.

"Because an innocent such as this one suffers the most through the trauma. They make the best soldiers. The fiercest!"

"Soldiers?" I watch this woman scream as her spirit gets torn out of her body. She doesn't deserve this. No one does. This is all my fault; I never should have gone through the astral dimension to find Ambrose. "Let her live," I scream as I watch the end of the spirit be driven out. The cashier's body slams to the floor with a hard thud, her lifeless body lying face down on the carpet.

I honestly don't know what prompts me to do it but I open my hand and let my dagger drop to the floor, its crash sounding distant in my ears. My eyes narrow on Rezmelda, with my hand out, palm facing her. The demoness flies back and hits the wall, cracking the drywall with her head.

"How are you doing this?"

Ignoring her, I run over to the spirit being consumed by the demoness's pouch. I open my crane bag and redirect the spirit to float inside. "This woman's spirit will not be a pawn to whatever plan your master has," I sneer.

NOT LIKE SHE'S HUMAN

ADDISON

Still pinned to the wall, Rezmelda squirms to get free. The rotting skin that had started at her hand is spreading to the rest of her arm and chest, reaching her neck as I force her to stay paralyzed.

Yes, this is perfect. I've taken Rezmelda's powers as my own and turned her body into her own personal prison. She thought she could use them against some poor, defenseless girl who has nothing to do with what's happening, now she'll pay for it. Rezmelda's eyes move frantically from side to side, a gurgling sound coming from her throat as she tries to speak.

Tying my crane bag with its leather drawstring in a tight knot, I get up from the floor and inch closer to Rezmelda.

"What were you saying about me reaching my full potential?"

Rezmelda's eyes fixate on me as I flick my wrist, making the demoness's head twist upward. Anymore, and her head'll snap off. The rotting keeps growing, downward now, toward her legs. Rezmelda's face is no longer enticing, her hair becoming prickly and straw-like.

"Are you ready to talk?"

Rezmelda tries parting her lips but can't; her eyes, pleading. I inch closer. Hot air escapes the demoness's nostrils as her eyes dart around the room. Moving my hand down a little, I return Rezmelda's ability to speak. She coughs a few times, dust coming out of her throat. I flinch and wipe my face.

"Who sent you?"

Rezmelda laughs. "You think you can get me to talk with your little parlor tricks? You can't even begin to imagine what torture is like—"

With another flick of my wrist, I twist her neck again, tighter this time. "Who are you collecting souls for? Is it for a higher-level demon?"

Dax comes up beside me. "You called the spirit a soldier before. Why?"

Rezmelda coughs a few times and then erupts into laughter.

"Which demon is it? Has to be some kind of prince or king. Is it Paimon?"

Rezmelda quiets for a second.

"It is Paimon, isn't it? I'm right, aren't I?"

"Is he the only Prince you can think of? Oh, you are such a child!" Rezmelda bursts out laughing once again.

I sigh and pick up my dagger off the floor. "I wonder what this will do." I touch the demon's rotting flesh with the tip of the dagger. Her skin tears apart upon its touch, releasing a black gas.

"Addison, torture?" I can feel his eyes boring into the back of my head, but I don't look back at him.

"It's not like she's human." I slide the dagger down Rezmelda's arms. "Are you going to tell me who sent you here?"

"*Not like she's human*?" Rezmelda spits in a mocking voice. "What do you think *you* are? You are just like me, and now you're hurting one of your own!"

My face twists. "I am not like you! I'm not going to ask again. Who sent you?" Like her? Fuck out of here, no I'm not.

Her lips curl and her eyes narrow, eyeing me up and down. "In fact, you're not the only one who's a demon, are you?" She smirks.

Squinting one eye, I cock my head back. "What the hell are you talking about?"

"I see what you have there," she says, nudging her chin down to my body.

"What?" I look down, confused.

Her eyes flick from side to side, searching my face. "Oh dear, dear, dear. You don't know, do you?"

"Know what?" She's stalling. I'm not entertaining this for long.

A gleam in her eye sparks. "My dear, have you been feeling ill lately?"

This causes me to quirk a brow.

"Bit of morning sickness, maybe?"

I part my lips, but before I can utter a sound, she says, "How about any cravings? No, not yet? Too soon maybe . . ."

My face pales. There's no way in hell she's suggesting that—No, how? My heart lunges to my throat as the sickening image of Azazel on top of me—Oh fucking hell! My breath grows shallow. I can't let her keep talking. If it's true, I'll need to find out myself. Even though I'm sure it isn't. She's just fucking with me, riling me up. But just in case, I can't let Dax hear it from her. I haven't told him I was practically raped by Azazel. He made me think I was with Ambrose . . .

"What's the matter, sweetie?" She spits with a hoarse tongue. "Hell bat's caught your tongue?"

My cheeks redden and I divert my attention back to my task. "I'm going to ask you one last time," I say, pointing the dagger tip forward. "Who commands you?"

She sneers and I lunge forward, aiming the dagger straight at the bitch's throat.

"Fine, I'll talk, I'll talk!" she says as she struggles to twitch herself free.

I lift my chin and narrow my brows at her.

"Under one condition."

"What's that?"

"Will you release me if I do? I promise I'll go straight back to LLAPS. But please don't kill me."

"Deal. Now, who sent you?"

"Let go of my neck first."

I hesitate, but if it's the only way to get her to talk, I have to. I wave my hand and release the demoness's neck, but still keep the rest of her pinned and paralyzed to the wall. I cross my arms, the dagger clutched in my left hand, while waiting for Rezmelda to stretch her neck and talk. Rezmelda locks eyes with the dagger, then with me.

"Well?"

Rezmelda cocks her head back and spits a green acid fluid right into my face. Spit flies out of my mouth and onto the floor. I gag. Skadi gets up to sniff what it is.

"Addison! Are you alright?" Dax yells.

My face burns while Rezmelda laughs hysterically, still unable to move. I lift a corner of my cloak and wipe my face with it. Itching increases as I struggle to get it all off. Skadi jumps up on my stomach and starts licking the acid from my neck and cheeks. My eyes are tightly shut as I manage to summon healing energy between my palms, bringing my emotions to a state I know wouldn't falter my spell, not that I need any help summoning rage this time. I don't know how an angry emotion would cause healing, but in my case, it does.

Skadi licks her lips as I push the hellhound back down to the floor, using her as a crutch to help myself up at the same time. "You'll pay for that."

Rezmelda has tears of blood rolling down her face from laughing so hard.

"But first, I have a question." Keeping my distance, I lift my hand once again, twisting the demon's neck. Rezmelda stops laughing and squints her eyes.

"Do demons have souls?" My lips curl upward and black vines grow from the ground, covering all of Rezmelda's rotting flesh. Her eyes are the only things emerging from between the plants. Screams fly out of her mouth as she's stunned to death. I swallow the poisonous insinuations running through my mind from what she had suggested and turn to my hellpup.

"Come here girl, lunchtime." Skadi flies past me and pounces right on top of the demoness, dragging her down from the wall. My lips lift to a smirk as I watch my hound rip right through the vines and into the rotting corpse of this demon.

I half turn to my brother while keeping watch. "Hey Dax, what happens to a demon's spirit if it dies here on Earth?"

"No idea. It goes back to LLAPS I suppose."

"Hmm, not if it gets eaten by a hellhound though." I hook my dagger back in my belt loop and look back up at Skadi, who's finishing up her meal. "Now, that's a good girl! That's what you're meant to eat." I touch my crane bag to make sure it's secure and that its new content is safe. My eyes fall to the poor cashier who fell victim to a demoness from LLAPS. "We can't let any more of these things happen."

"We best get a move on then," Dax says. Skadi finishes off the scraps left over and is sniffing the floor for anything else. I jump and run over to her.

"Wait, wait." I bend over and grab the pouch that belonged to Rezmelda, full of egregores. I pick it up and make sure it's closed tight before tucking it away in my pocket. "Can't let you eat all of these tasty sweets, now can I? Or I won't have anything to reward you with!" Or keep you in check.

Skadi approaches and starts sniffing at my pocket. I pat her head and scratch between the ears. "Are you ready for your next hunt?" That was exhilarating. A surge of energy tingles my skin. Despite the woman I couldn't save, at least her spirit is safe with me for the time being, and with what I just did—what I was able to do to that demoness . . . It makes me feel powerful.

"Are we ready?" Dax asks, already behind the broken glass window of the shop.

"Yep, coming. Come on, girl." This time, Skadi isn't going to leave my side, busy sniffing my pocket. She knows I have food, and she knows we're hunting.

"Are we going to talk about this?" Dax asks as I step over the glass.

I give him an inquisitive look. "Talk about what?"

Dax clears his throat and eyes the bookstore. "The torture. Didn't exactly seem like you."

I fall silent for a few minutes as we walk out of the small shopping area. I shake my head and scoff. "I mean, again, she wasn't human. I didn't know it would hurt her all that much. I was trying to get her to tell us who's commissioning for souls. And in case you weren't paying attention, she spat acid in my face."

"Not human, okay. Pretending what she said back there about you now being different doesn't matter, you wouldn't even torture a mouse."

I screw up my face. "Why would I torture a mouse?"

"Well, it isn't human."

"You're being silly. What does the CIA do with humans when they need answers, huh?"

Dax shifts uncomfortably. "You're going through many changes, Addie. I don't want you to change too much."

"I'm not."

Dax shoots me a look.

"I'm really not. I'm still the same Addison, just trying to fix this mess. Okay?" My voice cracks as I see the way he's looking at me. As if I'm becoming some kind of monster I can't control. It's not true though, and I know it. It's time to take matters into my own hands, and sometimes that calls for drastic measures. How else does he expect me to handle these powerful demons, if they aren't even going to respect me as their new Queen? Even if I'm just playing the part to get them to listen. I'm not going to stand by and let things happen.

Dax stays quiet and shrugs his shoulders. A few moments later he asks, "So, how did you know the dagger would do that to her? Make her release some black smoky gas?"

"I didn't, it was me the whole time. I wanted to make her think the dagger would be worse."

"You seem to have gotten better control of your new powers."

I nod. "Only when I'm angry though. And according to

Rezmelda, I haven't even reached my full potential. I mean, did you see how I absorbed her powers and poisoned her with them?"

Dax does a double-take. "Is *that* what you did?"

"Yeah, and how I grew vines from the ground and had them suffocate her to death." I shiver. "Come to think of it, maybe I did get a little carried away." I lower my eyes to the ruby hilt of the dagger. "Did you notice the way she looked at the dagger? I mean, at first I thought it was because she was scared of it, but it was almost as if she was waiting for the perfect moment to take it from me."

"If that's the case, you'll need to be careful not to drop it again."

I nod and tuck the dagger under my cloak.

Dax eyes me with one eye. "Well, that makes Earth."

"What do you mean?"

"The elements. The vines make Earth. I suppose all you need now is Air and you've unlocked your full potential."

My eyes shoot up. "Do you think that's what it'll take for me to get stronger?"

"Or strongest? Maybe. It's not like there's a guidebook, right?"

"No, I guess not." I flick down to Skadi, whose pointy ears perk up as she notices me looking at her. Such large ears, you could almost see down to her skull. "Alright Skadi, go find us another demon."

Reaching into Rezmelda's pouch, I let loose an opaque little bird. It hops to the ground, releasing fond memories as it pecks. Skadi licks it off the ground and swallows it whole. "Good girl, now go!" Skadi takes off in a half-run, half-glide north up a bridge. We follow closely behind her on the sidewalk as the dark purple smoke inches along the sky. The ocean waters next to us are rocky, rental boats tied up to a dock of Marty & Son's Boat Rentals smash on the choppy surface of the water. I take in the sea breeze, the smell of saltwater filling my nostrils. I gaze down at the crashing waves, a sense of familiarity waving over me, all except the cold temperature. A fish jumps up, splashing some cold water. At least the ocean isn't having to deal with demons taking their spirits. Guess there isn't a demon market for fish souls. However, how long till the change in climate kills them all? The purple sky is settled over our heads. I peer into the distance. At least there's a semblance of blue sky out there.

"Is the sky merging faster or slower? I can't tell."

Dax spins around, scanning our surroundings. "Shit, Addison look over there." He points toward the ocean to our left.

I swallow down hard. Revitalizers are catching up to us.

"Do you think they see us? Or are they scanning the area?"

"If they see us, they'd be coming toward us, I think." Dax rubs his chest and clears his throat.

"You okay?"

"Yeah, I'm fine. Let's hurry to the shopping center up ahead. It's where Skadi is leading us apparently."

It's a two-mile walk on the bridge until we reach the Ol' Mangrove shopping plaza. Skadi lowers her head, sniffing the ground with her tail pointing straight down, and begins to turn the corner. Out of habit, I place my left hand on the dagger, even though a part of me knows I probably don't need it anymore. The way I was able to kill Rezmelda without it taught me that.

Another shopping center, another ghost town. We reach the corner of the Winn-Dixie and stop to scan the perimeter. The fact that the blue sky is becoming the eerie purple of

LLAPS is no longer as unsettling as it is useful. For me to see spirits, anyway. My eyes stop at the little coffee shop with the poster of the grim reaper dancing with a flamingo. My lips curve into a smile. If only I knew the irony of that poster back then as I sat and had coffee and key lime pie with Ambrose. How much I didn't know, and how much I should have known if it wasn't for the fact I had a curse on me back then. I raise my hand to my chest and grab on to my necklace. *Ambrose.* A tear forms at the corner of my eye and I bite my tongue, shaking away memories from my mind. *I can't let myself think about that now.*

A low, deep growl escapes Skadi before prowling toward a tree right by the McDonald's. Dax and I jog behind her to keep up.

"This one's from LLAPS, Addison."

"How do you know?" I peer at what Skadi is stalking but can't yet see it.

"I just know, call it a reaper's hunch." He gets closer to the hellhound, trying not to make a sound while treading on the grass.

A desperate howling echoes from the shadows under the black olive tree. The hairs at the back of my neck prickle my skin as I recognize the sound the spirit made. It's the same noise the bodiless heads with hollowed eyes and gaping mouths made at the level of LLAPS Azazel had shown me from the suicides. Lost souls stuck floating in self-loathing and despair. My heart sinks. I move in closer behind Skadi, trying not to alert anyone. The last thing I want is for Skadi to get angry, or for the spirit to become translucent or float away. The poor being has imprisoned itself inside of its own torment in LLAPS, never to escape, never to obtain the knowledge of being able to rise above its torment and leave. How did it know to go through the portal though? And now it's in danger of being consumed, one way or another, with no chance of redeeming itself. I can't let that happen.

"You're going to have to be quick about this, Addie."

"Hush, I'm trying."

"Yeah well, *they* don't seem to care about that."

I lift my head to see three revitalizers circling high above us. "Shit." I grab the pouch full of egregores and let out two in the opposite direction and away from the spirit. Distracted by the sudden free food, Skadi shifts her attention and makes a dash for them. The oval head comes back into view, disfigured while collapsing and lengthening in size due to it not having a structure. It looks back at me with saddened, hollow eyes and moans. Distressed. Dissolved in fear.

"Shhh, come here. I've got you." I open the crane bag, luring the spirit in by inching closer. "Come on, in you go."

"Addison?"

"Dax, I can't move any faster. I don't want it to—" I sigh as the bodiless spirit backs away from me and Dax. "Float away." I glance at Skadi, who's now licking her lips and ready to pounce on her previous hunt. "Oh no, you don't. Dax, can you manage the other bag?"

Dax grabs Rezmelda's bag from my hand and opens it.

"Be careful not to let them all out."

A few egregores whoosh out of the bag and scatter around the pavement. A mushroom grows a pair of legs and starts to run, while an ugly goblin-looking thing smiles from pointy ear to pointy ear and grabs an egregore rabbit by the throat. This is enough to entertain Skadi while I inch closer to the floating head. I push the crane bag closer, unsure of how the other spirit knows to stay in, and fearful of it escaping. The hollowed eyes follow the bag, as the revitalizers swarm closer.

"Addie—they're getting closer," he says with urgency in his voice.

The head floats away from the tree.

"No, come back here! I'm trying to help you," I say in a loud whisper. Skadi, who has gulped down the last of her treats, turns with a snarling growl.

"Addison, I think it's time to let that one go."

"Are you kidding me? I've almost got it."

"Seriously though, we're severely outnumbered."

Hesitant to keep my eye off the floating spirit, I turn my neck an inch. Dax is right. We *are* surrounded. I get up off the grass as more black voided figures circle around us. A few of them float down at a fast speed. We inch back. I shoot a glance at the spirit, just to see where it went, but it hasn't moved. It probably doesn't even know of the danger it's in.

A revitalizer looms right over my back, engulfing me with sorrowful rage.

Images of Ambrose swim inside my mind again. Annoyed, I shake off the memories. I'm not going to let myself be victim to them again. I've pulled away from them before, I can do it again and it's becoming easier and easier each time. Darkness reaches every corner of my mind with ease, and I'm able to pull myself free from their paralyzing hold. I spot another revitalizer closing in on the spirit, so I leap to the ground like a cat. Crane bag open, I manage to force the floating head inside. My shoes skid on the grass as I struggle to keep my balance, slamming my butt to the ground. Dax comes up beside me, grabbing my arm and helping me up.

The three of us take off at a full sprint. We follow Skadi if not to the next location, as far away as we can possibly run from the revitalizers. We leave the plaza's parking lot and run into the street past a dozen or so gumbo limbo trees. The purple sky has reached this far too. Just when we think we're ahead of the revitalizers, we come face to face with a blind guardsman.

ALWAYS THE LAST TO KNOW

ADDISON

Skadi ducks in panic as she backs away from the guardsman's swinging ax. Poor hellhound. Back at LLAPS, she'd flee the scene without a second thought. My guess is she doesn't want to leave us—me. I leap in and grab onto her neck, tugging her away as she lunges back, lifting off the ground, taking me with her. I catch a few feet of air when my brother grabs onto my waist and brings me down. I let go of Skadi as Dax rushes me to a nearby overgrown bush by the pavement. Holding my breath, I stay still, my eyes on Skadi as she follows suit, her head low and now by my side. Smart as shit, this one. I suspected it before, but now I'm sure of it. Another dog would have kept whimpering and making a fuss. Skadi knows she's mine now and can tell what's going on. The more I learn about her, the more I understand how hellhounds operate. Dax holds a finger to his mouth as I grip Skadi's head to keep her from making any noise, just in case.

The guardsman lifts its large eyeless cone of a head and sniffs the air. I exhale slowly as it lowers its head and takes a few forward strides. That's right, keep moving sucker. No one's here. Maybe being on Earth is too alien for the guardsman to claim its bearings. A few minutes pass as we wait by the bush and watch as the guardsman takes its sweet time, securing every inch of its location. Meanwhile, revitalizers close in. They're getting closer, with no place for us to run even if we tried. We're sitting ducks.

Skadi's tail starts to hit the ground in anticipation. Okay, maybe not that smart. I know she wants to fly out but she's going to have to wait a little longer. I trap her tail under my foot to keep it from moving and Skadi locks eyes with me, her pupils red and dilating. "Shhhh . . . calm down, girl."

I bite down on my tongue as something vibrates from inside my cloak. My heart comes to a full stop as I dart my eyes to the guardsman.

"What the hell is that?" Dax shoots me a fierce look. Son of a bitch, it's my phone.

"Turn that off," Dax whispers as I give him an apologetic look. I fumble under my cloak as the vibration continues. Shit, shit, shit! Who can be calling me? It's coming from my pocket, not my cloak! I pull it out and drop my mouth. It's Ava!

"Turn it off, Addison!"

Quickly hitting the end call button, I stuff it back in my pocket. Too late. The guardsman turns around with its ax pulled up over our heads.

Just great.

Thinking fast, I fill my power with rage, just like I did before, drawing it out through my arms, and out toward the guardsman. Hot energy surfaces from the pit of my gut, warming me and causing my palms to heat up as I let it all out. The guardsman lowers its ax and I lower my arms a smidge.

"I think I stopped it."

"What did you do?"

"I'm not sure. I couldn't decide what it is exactly, so I didn't know what to do. I just sent out a spell to make it stop."

The guardsman starts to shake.

"Wait, what's happening?" Dax asks, urgency in his voice.

Holy fuck . . . I stumble back, prickling the side of my arm with the leaves behind me.

The guardsman's head shakes vigorously until his entire body trembles and I think he's about to explode when—it duplicates itself. It fucking duplicates itself.

Now there are two of them.

They both raise their axes over their pale conical heads at the same time and proceed to glide toward us.

"Run!" Dax yells, pushing me to the side. Skadi scurries to get her tail from beneath my feet without tripping over my cloak. Dax holds out his hand to keep me from falling as Skadi lunges in front of us, pushing me out of the way as one of the guardsmen swings its ax. We bolt across the street after Skadi. At least there aren't any cars. I glance behind me. The guardsmen are picking up speed, their steel axes gliding over the asphalt like they would at LLAPS.

"Dax, we have to lose them."

"Yeah but how?"

"I thought Skadi could eat guardsmen." My heart is panting hard as I keep a fast-running pace, only looking back to see how far they are. The guardsmen are catching up at a supernatural speed, swinging their axes with every stride.

"No, they share the corridors but ignore each other. Addison, over there!" I look to where he's pointing as we reach a clearing of bushes and mangroves swaying in the coastal breeze. A small speed boat is tied off to the side.

"What? The boat? Are you crazy? We'll be trapped!"

"You got any better ideas? Use it to hide."

I reach the boat and put one leg on the stairs to help me up while Skadi follows and hops inside. Once inside, I turn around and hold out a hand to Dax.

"I'm not coming. I'll be back."

"What? What are you going to do?"

"Just stay in the cabin and be quiet."

I open my mouth to speak but Dax is already jogging away. I grab Skadi and duck inside the cabin. I peer through the window but can't see my brother through the mangroves. What could he possibly do to a guardsman?

Skadi rummages through the boat's interior as I struggle to stick my head out the window. I bring my neck back in to control my antsy hellbeast when my phone begins to vibrate again. This time I answer.

"Hello, Ava?"

"Girl, where have you been? I've been trying to get a hold of you!"

"Ava, are you okay? How's it looking in Miami?"

"It's weird, Addison! People have been acting strange and disappearing. My grandpa told me this had to do with the other side. And that you weren't okay. Girl, *what* is going on?"

I stick my knee between Skadi and the flapping doors that lead to the cupboards while switching my phone to my other ear. Skadi starts to growl. "Shh."

"What was that? Did you get a dog?"

"Sorry, I'm kind of in the middle of, uh . . . a lot has happened since I last saw you. So, you say there are still people out there?"

"Yeah, there are still people, what are you talking about?"

"But they're acting weird. Weird, like how? Ava, *how* are they acting weird?"

"I don't know, just incoherent, like zombies sort of. Why, how's it looking in the Keys?"

"Not good. No one is around. It's a ghost town. Ava, listen to me. I don't have time to explain everything but a portal was opened on the other side, and a shit ton of demons escaped. And spirits too, but I'm trying to help those." Ava falls silent on the other end. "Ava? Are you there?"

"Y–yes, I'm here. Addison . . . My grandpa said something similar. That's why I called. He's warding the house, he said you've changed somehow. Is that true?"

I grip onto the phone tightly and hold my breath. You have no idea. But there's no time for me to explain everything to her right now.

Behind me, a bright blue light illuminates the outside. I glance down at my necklace. But it isn't glowing. What the hell was that? I know Dax doesn't have his scythe . . .

"Addison? Are you there?"

"I, um, have changed. I have some new powers. But I really can't talk now. Ava, you need to stay safe. Whatever you do, do not go outside. Stay within Padrino's warding."

"Wait, don't go! Changed how? My grandpa wanted me to tell you something."

"What?"

"He says to tell you that you need to take control. Make it neutral. What does that mean?"

My eyebrows furrow as my gaze drops to the phone. *Neutral?*

"Addison—he says that if you don't . . . something really bad will happen. Do you know what he means?"

"No idea. I really have to go now. I'll call you soon." Without waiting for a response, I click end call. The rocking of the boat makes me turn around to see my brother stepping inside. He taps Skadi on the head as he climbs down the steps. "That was Ava."

"She was the one calling before too?"

I nod my head. "She says people are acting weird in Miami, and slowly disappearing. I didn't have time to explain everything to her but that means things are slowly progressing."

"Right, as opposed to how quickly people stopped coming out of their homes here."

My frown deepens. "Dax, I saw a blue light again before you came in. But my necklace definitely didn't glow." I clench my jaw, holding back my tears.

"Oh, that?" Dax shifts from one foot to the other and scratches his head. "Yeah . . . uhh . . . that was me."

I raise a brow and flick my eyes up.

He lets out a long, winded sigh.

"What are you talking about?"

He pulls out his scythe from his coat and my lips part. "You got it back . . ." When did he get it back? "Wait a minute . . . the blue light from before . . . Dax . . . why didn't you tell me?"

"I'm sorry Addie," he tucks his scythe back in his coat and drops his hands. "Deacon visited me while you were napping and told me not to tell you . . ."

"Tell me what? Dax, what are you not telling me?" My stomach curdles as the expression on his face drops. Something terrible has happened. I can feel it in my bones.

He rubs the back of his neck and his eyes fall to the ground. "Addie . . ."

"What is it? Dax, what the hell? Just tell me. What's going on?"

"Ambrose . . . he–he's alive."

My chest tightens and my stomach flips. "What?" is all I can mutter. All this time I thought he was dead. "But . . . he died in my arms . . ."

"And then Deacon shrouded her arms over him as she opened a portal to the Akashic. She told me he was brought back to life, fully, reaper powers and all."

Now my stomach lurches. *Ambrose is alive!* My heart pounds heavily in my chest as I steady myself toward the door.

"Where are you going?"

"To open a portal to go see my boyfriend. Where do you think?"

"Wait." He blocks the door. "What about saving the people here?"

"Well, why not do that with him?"

"Addie . . . I can't let you go to him."

"Can't let me? What are you talking about? Get out of my way, Dax." He shakes his head slowly and my eyes narrow. "Why didn't you tell me Deacon came to visit you? And why didn't you tell me Ambrose was alive before?"

His eyes search mine and I can tell he's scrambling for his words.

"Dax, do not lie to me. Why didn't you tell me Ambrose was alive?"

He opens his mouth and closes it. "Ambrose is kind of . . . not allowed anywhere near you at the moment, and the reapers are hunting demons." He snaps his mouth shut again.

"Hunting demons?"

"With orders to kill on sight. They believe anyone who escaped the prisons is up to no good."

My throat dries and my knees quiver against the rocking of the boat. I grab onto Skadi as she leans her weight into my leg. "And Ambrose isn't allowed to see me?"

"They're keeping him really busy. The only reason I'm here with you is because Deacon knows you're in danger. At least I can keep you safe from the other reapers."

I run my hand through my hair. This is a lot to take in. Still, though, it's not like Ambrose to obey orders and not come find me. Wouldn't that be the first thing he would do? To at least let me know he's alive . . . ? Wait—"Is Deacon the new Judge?" She was next in line, wasn't she?

Dax stills. "Mmhm . . . yep."

"That makes sense. So, why keep him from me, and why not just tell the other reapers not to kill me?"

Dax shifts uncomfortably. "I think she's trying her best, Addie. But she needs you out of the way to keep you from danger. I'm sorry. This is the way it has to be."

Something still isn't sitting right with me. Skadi growls.

"We should go." Dax turns toward the door.

"So, those guardsmen . . . You blasted them with your scythe?"

"Yes, it was the only way to get rid of them and I didn't have time to think."

"Speaking of time to think," I say in attempts to distract myself from my thoughts, "you saw how I accidentally duplicated the guardsman?"

"Yes, how'd you manage that?"

"Guess I wasn't specific enough. Didn't have time to think, as you said."

"Well, looks like you need more practice then. We

should get a move on before revitalizers surround the boat, or more guardsmen show up."

"Sure." I grab onto the countertop as the boat rocks back and forth, balancing myself as I step onto the stairs leading out.

"Addie, you okay? You look a little flushed . . ."

"Well, why wouldn't I look flushed? I just learned that— Uh . . ." Bile rises to my throat. "Oh no, oh no, oh no." My steady walk becomes a brisk jog as I push the cabin doors open and lunge myself over the boat. Dax grabs me from behind to keep me from falling overboard as my guts once again spew in chunks, all over the boat's white gelcoat exterior.

EXISTENTIAL AMBROSE

AMBROSE

"Your reports are ready."

"Give me a summary," I say, unflinching from my hard stare at the slate. She has her arms extended, holding a thick folder in her hand. After a moment she takes it back and clears her throat.

"The corridors are being cleared of any loose prisoners. I have put reapers to assist as some have learned to outsmart the guardsmen." Her eyes burn on the back of my head, waiting for a reply. I keep my eyes glued to the glistening waters of the Akashic pond in my new quarters, watching as calming ripples hit the surface toward me. The weight of my scythe against my shrouded shoulder, a constant reminder of my newly given burden and responsibility. Reapers can't fraternize with humans. No matter how many times I push those words to the back of my mind, they always come back.

Even though I intend to change things and have stated it to the council, a silence falls around me whenever I'm in the vicinity of the other reapers. I know they don't approve, and I know I shouldn't care. But I do. If we're meant to all work together, create a bond among reapers, is it wise to start leading with them hating me? Perhaps it was too soon to declare all of my intentions.

When I don't say anything, she lowers her eyes and flips open the folder. "We have reapers out on Earth taking care of the humans who are dying, Dax being one of them."

Dax. I had avoided scrying for his whereabouts, not wanting to look for Addison. Not that I don't want to but ignoring my instincts to do so. With Deacon continuously leering over me, afraid my attention is split—which it is, I can't stop thinking about her—and the constant reminder that I have a huge task in front of me, searching for him would break a seal. Cause me to obsess. What if she isn't safe and with him? What if she was with him, while he reaps and demons intervene? Swallowing hard, I adjust my scythe on my shoulder. She saw me get killed. It's best she thinks me dead and moves on with her life. Fact of the matter is, Deacon has always been right. Not about reapers not being able to spend time with humans, getting to know them, their habits, what makes them love, what makes them tick. Those things would create a world where reapers care for humans, making them more sympathetic, thus actually easing their pain when they cross over. Instead of lending a stone-cold hand, hardly any explanation, adding to the fury and resentment they leave earth with. None of it is fair. Why should we add to their pain when we should be easing it?

But having actual relationships, intimate, sexual. It does complicate things. At least for me it does—will. As the new Judge. Not that I would reprimand another reaper if one is to fall in love with a human. I'm not a hypocrite. But finding Addison now would severely complicate things for me, for us.

I can't lead a council of reapers, oversee everything, and

also have a girlfriend. I cannot afford for my attention to be split. Distracted. I have no choice but to let her go, no matter how much of me yearns for her and wants her by my side. She is human after all and should be given the freedom to live a normal life, get married, have babies, that sort of thing. All I'll end up doing is distract her from living the life she should be living. And I can't be selfish, I see that now.

"Don't go scrying for Addison, Ambrose. There's much at stake here. Keep focus." Deacon snaps my attention back to the present and I remark with a grunt.

"All I do is keep focus, Deacon." I straighten up my collar, still looking out to the rippling effects of the water, and casually glance in her direction, softening my features. She should have had this position. She's only trying to do right by the council and make sure earth doesn't break into an apocalypse while at the same time worried I might crack from all my human baggage. "What of the prisoners who escaped? Any of them caught yet?

"A few."

"And?"

"Killed, as you ordered." Her last word scratchy as she shuts the folder closed.

"Good."

"Ambrose, without a legion, it is only natural for demons to run amok. Won't you consider creating a plan to solely call them back? Instead of killing them off?"

I grunt and turn my back toward her. "They know what they're doing. Don't think them innocent, Deacon. If they escaped, it was to raise havoc on earth. If they were smart, they'd come back. Let us not forget who they looked up to before, and how all this started."

"Yes. Azazel." She sighs.

"Since when did you care about the well-being of

demons, anyway?"

Deacon parts her lips, probably taken aback that I snapped at her. I usually never unleash my temper at her. Normally I can keep my head cool, but she out of all people should know how I feel about demons right now. And the prisoners? The disgusting scum doing who knows what up on earth—only to hurt Addison and any other innocent up there. Even still, I couldn't do this without Deacon. To be fair, if it wasn't for her, I don't know if I would have been able to assume my position at all.

"Deacon I–I want you to know I do appreciate you. Everything you do and stand for. I'm just—dealing with all this the best way I can."

She nods, a tiny glimpse of a sideways smile on her lips, and then it's gone. "But not all those prisoners out there knew of Azazel's plan and deserve to be wiped out of existence," she continues, and I turn back to the waters, letting out an inaudible sigh. "There's absolutely no point in expending reaper power in collecting them and bringing them back. None. Why keep them suffering for eternity anyway? Why not instead release their energy to the ether to be reused? Seems like a better use of their energy, as a matter of fact." She pauses for a few beats and I snap my gaze back to her.

"I know, Ambrose. I'm here for you. No matter what you decide to do. I fully accept knowing I'll be doing damage control with any repercussions."

I scoff but then return her smile before she continues. I do take solace in knowing I'll always have her by my side. What a long way we've come.

"The demons who left, however," she stammers, "have proven to be a bit trickier. We're hoping the revitalizers and guardsmen do a better job at collecting them."

My frown deepens and I gaze back down at the waters, tilting the scythe forward a little to make the surface of the water begin to change color. From a crystal blue to dark, almost black. A few seconds later, an image of dark purple clouds surface.

"Show me how far the purple clouds have spread."

The image expands in the water, forming a map. I squint to where the purple clouds are circulating. "Why only in this one spot?" Deacon doesn't respond.

Tilting my scythe again, I zoom the image larger into the concentrated area for a better look. The purple clouds are circling over Tavernier Key, and it's growing. This is precisely why I've avoided scrying. "Prisoners and demons didn't just escape to Earth, they escaped to where Addison is."

"I promise you, we're taking care of it, Ambrose," Deacon says rapidly, now pushing her way in front of me. "It's better that we keep it concentrated for now. So that the problem doesn't get larger."

"What's this?" My brows knit together as I push Deacon from my view, ignoring the fact that she knew what was going on. She turns to look as well.

A large demon shows up on the map. This time, I open my hand, drawing the image even closer. It's in a hospital, surfacing a sick boy.

"What is he doing to that child?"

My jaw drops as the demon opens up its round mouth and starts sucking out the boy's soul. Deacon jolts back.

I grip my scythe. "I'm going down there."

"Wait, I can delegate—"

"No, I'm taking care of this myself."

Deacon backs up, letting me pass. "You go on ahead, there's something I need to take care of first."

HEAD CAGE

ADDISON

Third time I've vomited since I've been back.

I help myself to a water bottle inside the boat's mini-fridge, rinse my mouth out, and wipe my face. I feel like a cotton ball has been jabbed down my throat. Maybe Rezmelda was right. Ugh. Even thinking that makes my stomach churn. Like when you're about to be fired, or it's a matter of days until the house foreclosure notice comes in the mail. Or worse, when the doctor comes out of surgery with a grim look on his face, and you know your brother didn't make it.

"Woah. Easy, Addie. Steady."

"Thanks." I grab his hand and he helps me onto steady land, though the ground sways under my feet.

"You okay?"

"I, uh—yeah, fine," I lie. Of course, I can confide in Dax, but I'm not ready to face the music yet. A part of me is still hoping this is all just nerves. Like when I threw up in LLAPS.

I was revolted, absolutely disgusted.

Maybe I'm not over the shock yet, as much as I want to

be, and my mind and body aren't up to speed. The cotton ball grows as if telling me, "Nope, you're wrong. Rezmelda's right."

Fuck you, cotton ball.

"I thought you said you were feeling better?"

When did I say that? "I don't know. Guess I'm still feeling off after coming back from LLAPS." I shrug. Dax nods, his brows knitted together as he studies me, so I turn on my heel and start walking.

A crash explodes in the distance. A little ways away from the Ol' Mangrove shopping center we were at.

"What the hell was that?"

Dax places his hand on my upper back, pushing me in the opposite direction. "Most likely another guardsman."

"No, wait, there might be more spirits in danger. Or worse, people," I sputter. "Dax, what are you doing?"

"You're joking, right? Addie, you just threw up. Let's get you back inside and I'll go handle this."

"Hell no! Absolutely not. I'm going. I'm fine Dax, really." He might have his scythe, but I'm not defenseless! Hello? Half demon! And besides, it was my idea to save these spirits! No way he's benching me.

Skadi crouches like she's hunting and itching for a chase. More crashing erupts and she takes off full speed ahead, kicking up dust as her claws eat the dirt.

No time to lose. I speed after her, hoping I don't get dizzy from the run.

"Addison, wait." Dax reaches for my arm. "We don't know what we're going up against. We need to strategize. We're being reckless."

"But we need to get all of these spirits safe from the demons."

"Not like this."

I reach into Rezmelda's pouch and pull out a few egregores. "You're right." I toss them to the ground and Skadi halts, distracted. The crashing gets louder. "We're nearby. If it's more guardsmen, what do you suppose we do?"

"Well, we shouldn't be running toward them."

"But what if there are people in danger?" I point toward the chaotic noises. "It sounds like it's coming from where I work." As those words roll off my tongue, the truth of it strikes me in the chest. My coworkers and patients are still in there. Why hadn't I thought of them sooner? With so much going on at once, I guess I pushed my mundane life and job to the back of my mind.

"Dax . . . I have to get there. I can handle the demons like I handled Rezmelda, you handle the guardsmen."

Dax's forehead crinkles and he sighs, dropping his arms. As he opens his mouth to speak, Skadi growls deep and menacing and takes off again.

"Skadi, come back!" I reach into the pouch, but nothing comes out. Oh shit. It's empty. I gasp and run after the hellhound.

"Addison, wait!"

I ignore him, not wanting to lose sight of Skadi. He needs to get with the program; what's the matter with him?

"Addison, we're running toward danger. Can we stop?"

Skadi halts in front of a concrete building. Seashore Memorial. As far as hospitals are concerned, this one is small; only four stories.

"Addison, wait." His voice is deep and hoarse. Assertive.

I purse my lips and turn to face him. "I'm sorry, Dax. I didn't want to lose Skadi."

Dax points at the sky. A deep purple vortex spins above the hospital.

"It's getting worse," I say.

"Means more guardsmen and revitalizers are coming out. The demons are the least of our problems."

"I don't care, Dax. This town is in trouble. If we don't do something, this concentrated little issue will spread. Look how far it's come!" I pull open the hospital doors and walk inside, cool wind from the air conditioning hitting my face.

"There's power."

"Probably the backup generator. Any idea how long it'll last before the monitors and stuff start to shut down?" Dax asks.

I shake my head. My throat and chest ache at the thought of the hospital losing power. What will I do about the patients?

"Where do we start?"

The crashing sounds come back, harder this time, and I startle. Skadi huffs and pushes open the double doors leading to the infirmary, Dax and I following behind her.

The neon overhead lights flicker down the hallway. Besides Skadi's claws scraping across the floor, it's quiet. Almost too quiet. We make our way down the corridor, passing a utility closet and a small office. The next window belongs to a hospital room and I approach with caution. It's pitch-black inside. As I approach the bed, my hand flies to my heart. "We're too late."

I gaze down at a middle-aged woman with a cast on her leg.

"She was here for a broken leg? She could have survived!" I pull my hair back and take in a heavy breath, closing my eyes.

A thunderous crash, as if pots and pans are being thrown into a wall, makes my hands shake.

"We should go, Addie."

"How many of these rooms are there going to be? Full of, of . . ." Dead bodies. Probably all of them.

Dax shakes his head and walks out of the room. I'm about to follow when I notice Skadi is nowhere to be seen. I spin around. Uh oh . . .

"Dax? Where's Skadi?" I scan the room and rush out, gaze skimming each side of the corridor.

"Oh shit, she must have wandered off hunting!"

"What if there's a guardsman or revitalizer?"

Dax shrugs. "Honestly, would it be so bad if we lose her?"

My jaw drops. "Are you serious? We need her to hunt!"

"Do we? The city is swarming with stuff. I'm sure we could do fine without her. She's kind of holding us back. And besides, how are you going to control her? She's eaten all of the egregores."

"I can make more!"

"Admit it, you want to keep her, don't you?" Dax crosses his arms.

"Well, yes. Don't you?"

"Addison, when all of this is over, you cannot keep a hellhound around the *house*. Someone will notice a flying large dog with glowing red eyes."

I suppress the urge to laugh. "So then I'll put a cloaking spell on her."

"Oh, and you can do that now?"

"I haven't tried, but I have new powers. I'm sure I can figure it out. Besides, who's to say I'll be staying home? I'm *queen* of LLAPS, remember?" I walk past him, leaving him gaping. My lips curl upward.

Alright, here we go again. I open the door to the next room on the left side of the hall. The lights are also out in here. A bald, old man lies lifeless on the bed, his head lulling to the side.

"Dead." I swallow hard, shaking my head, and duck out of the room, shutting the door on the way.

"Why don't I do a quick sweep for any survivors instead of checking every room?"

I cross my arms. "Right, since you've had your scythe this whole time. Remember, I'm also keeping an eye out for Skadi."

Dax winces. "Addie..."

"No it's fine. Good idea then, scan for any survivors. I'm going to keep walking and searching for our hellhound."

"Your hellhound."

I ignore him and start down the hallway alone. Another crash erupts from the floor above. I push another set of doors open but there's no sign of Skadi. Just dark room after dark room. I keep my eyes looking straight ahead; I know they're all dead. It's apparent that whatever demon is taking souls from the patients in the hospital has already cleared the first floor.

Broken chairs lie out scattered on a waiting area I approach. The vending machines are out of power, and one of them is toppled over with glass shards all over the tile. The generator must be reaching its end. I step inside to inspect the scene. Framed posters with images of the beach, broken on the floor, with glass shattered everywhere.

What could have done this?

Broken glass cracks beneath my boots as I carefully step around the area. A burning aroma assaults my nostrils and I spin around, looking for any sign of a fire. Another crash shakes the walls, closer and followed by furious barking.

"Skadi!" I take off, passing two stalled elevators. I blow through two sets of double doors until I reach the emergency exit. The stench of urine and something burning sears at my nose hair. I cup my hand over my nose and mouth and run up the stairs, swinging open the third-floor emergency door and dashing inside. My breath comes out with a loud whoosh. I come face to face with a familiar black jacket and a more welcoming smell of tobacco.

"Dax!"

"Hey, I came up here during my sweep. Are you okay?"

"Yes, what'd you find?"

"Everyone's dead on this floor. And I found something . . ."

I clench my jaw. "What is it?"

"I'm not sure if this is a good time to tell you . . ."

"Spit it out, Dax. We don't have time."

He lets out a shallow breath and reaches for my arm. "Follow me," he whispers.

I let him lead the way to a small supply closet. My heart pounds in my chest. "What's in here?"

He hesitates as he puts his hand on the doorknob and twists it open. "Brace yourself."

My eyes well with tears, but not enough to blur out the sight of five of my coworkers' bodies, cold and dead, huddled and clutching each other.

"They must have gone in here to hide."

My knees quiver and I drop to the floor. It's one thing sucking up the dread of seeing people I don't know suffer and die at the hands of demons, but another when it's my own coworkers. How long ago did this happen?

I should have been here. I should have thought of checking my job first.

All these patients, dead; my coworkers, dead, because of me. Because I didn't think of coming to a hospital when demons were taking souls from the living.

I catch my breath and swallow my tears. Dax places his hand on my shoulder and gently nudges me when the crashing happens again. I wish I could ignore it.

"Addison, you have to pick yourself up. Be strong, we have to keep going."

"Dax, I . . ."

"I know, but now is not the time to mourn. We have to keep going." I climb to my feet, wiping away my tears.

"Did you find any survivors?" I fight to keep my voice from cracking but fail.

"Yes, that's why we must go. All the way to the fourth floor. Come on."

"Okay."

He takes the lead as we climb two sets of stairs and I try to remember who would be working that wasn't in that closet. I grimace at the image of my coworkers huddled together, afraid for their lives. I have no idea what anyone's shifts are; I don't even know what day it is. Anyone could be up there.

When we reach the top of the stairs, fearsome growls echo from the other side of the door. I fly past Dax and fling it open.

"Addison, wait!"

Skadi looks up and wags her tail. She's licking her lips as if she had just finished gobbling down a tasty treat.

"Skadi, there you are! Come here." I reach over to grab her when the crashing shakes the walls. A long low moan follows after, sounding like it's coming from someone in pain. Skadi turns her large head and starts whipping her tail from side to side, slashing a cut on my leg as it smacks me.

"What the hell is doing that?" I take a few steps forward, shoving Skadi to the side with my hip.

"Addison, wait. Maybe you should let me go first."

Ignoring him, I pick up speed to where the moaning and cashing sounds keep coming from. Whatever it is, it killed my friends. And now it's going to pay. I inch closer to the room. A flickering yellow-green aura seeps out from beneath the door as I near.

I see red. A burning emotion resonates from my core, sending energy sparking up my arms.

Stay in control.

I try stabilizing my breathing but images pop into my head, reminding me why I'm angry. After what I've seen, I don't want to control it.

The door is open. Something rattles inside, but before I enter, something catches my attention. A floating cloak hovers over another hospital bed in the room across from me diagonally. If that's the demon, what's in here? I turn back to the room with the dim, flickering lights, and gasp.

A giant of a man sits on his haunches. His bald head is trapped by an iron cage. Spikes pierce his skin and dried blood crusts over his wounds. All the rage I felt before stepping into this room is replaced by panic. His cage rattles as he stares straight at me. Pleas don't resonate in this man's gaze. Instead, he narrows his eyes, his nostrils flare as he lets out a growl and stands. I back up toward the open door and he stomps toward me.

The walls and floor shake.

Dax pulls me away from the caged man's reach.

"What the hell is that?" I yell.

"A prisoner." Dax extends his arm, pushing me behind him.

"Wait, Dax, no. Let me try to help him."

The prisoner barges through the wall, sending dust and debris cascading down on us. "Dax, I almost forgot! The demon, he's in the last room!"

"What?"

Skadi jumps from behind us, her mouth wide open, and flies toward the prisoner.

"Skadi, no!" I call, wishing I had managed to make more egregores before getting up here. The way she gulped down the giant scorpion, twice the size of this giant, I have to grab her before she fills herself with this guy.

The prisoner flings his arm and Skadi drops onto her back, landing on the tile floor with a thud and a yelp. I wince. Ouch . . .

"Skadi!"

Skadi gets up, her tail low and not moving, her head down but red eyes gleaming as she snarls.

"She's okay," Dax says. "Stay behind me."

"Skadi," I whisper. "Go eat the demon." Skadi tilts her head, listening to my voice but not wanting to take her eyes off the prisoner.

"The demon, go eat the demon." I point to the back of the hallway. The prisoner shakes his head furiously, rattling the cage.

"Dax, how do we help him? He's pissed off and in pain. If we take that thing off of him, maybe he'll calm down!"

The prisoner yells and rushes forward, taking down a corner of the wall.

"Duck!" Dax screams as he places his hand on my head, forcing me down.

"Stop it, Dax, I can take care of myself!" I back away as the prisoner crashes into the emergency exit door. I turn, my back facing the hallways, keeping my eyes on the prisoner. I fumble for the crane bag. Trying not to let any of the other prisoners escape, I open it a little toward the prisoner.

"Come on, it's okay." I motion to the prisoner, trying to show him he can trust me.

The prisoner stops for a moment and looks at me, saliva drooling out of his mouth as metal spikes poke into his throat and cheeks. Whatever did you do to receive this fate? He shifts his attention down at the bag and then back up at me, and then Dax.

"That's right, a little closer." I step forward. The prisoner jumps back, its caged head hitting the door behind him. Blood spurts out from his head which makes him jump and dash forward. He extends his arms, trying to reach for me, but he doesn't look like he's going to go quietly.

"Addison, just take him like that." The cage rattling muffles his voice.

"What?"

"Trap him in the bag!"

"No! Help me pin him down so we can take the cage off him!"

"Are you crazy?"

I concentrate on all the anger and sadness I can muster, not that I need any help at this point. I need to be strong enough to hold this prisoner down. I open my hand and hold it out, palm facing the prisoner, who is charging ahead.

Skadi flies through the air and grabs onto the prisoner's arm with her teeth, chomping down hard. The crushing sound of his bones sends chills down my spine.

"Oh no, Skadi!" I lunge forward and cling to Skadi's backside, trying to pull her away, when the prisoner's eyes glow a bright yellow. He swings his arm upward, sending Skadi flying for the second time. Then he turns toward me and flings his other arm, hitting me right across the chest. I see stars as I sail through the air, and pain radiates down my legs as I crash on top of a broken table in one of the rooms.

LORCAN IS A DIRTBAG

ADDISON

*D*ax lifts a part of the table that had collapsed on top of me when I landed on it. He grabs my arms and lifts me up.

"You okay?"

My legs wobble as I try to stand, my head fuzzy and disoriented. Dax grips onto my arm, keeping me steady. I blink the room into view, the back of my head throbbing. "Yeah, I'm fine."

"The prisoner is out of control. I say we leave him and try to move past him. Let Skadi or a revitalizer finish him."

Of course he would say that. "The prisoner is in pain and doesn't know what he's doing. We're not leaving him—Shit, Dax, the demon!" I jump over the broken desk on the floor and poke my neck around the door frame. The prisoner ran into a wall and is banging his head inside one of the rooms. I spot Skadi on the far end of the hall, who's focusing on the demon's room. I beckon for Dax to follow. Keeping my eye on the prisoner, I move swiftly across the hall.

"Skadi, come here," I whisper. For a moment the prisoner stops. I crane my neck. He's staring back at me with wide eyes. I gulp. Dax starts to pull my arm back when Skadi growls, making the prisoner jump. He shakes his bald head furiously and screams. It's a deep, hoarse moan. He backs up in preparation to charge at us when my hands begin to warm. Okay, let's try this again . . .

A gust of wind blows through my hair and the prisoner's eyes widen. A smile creeps onto my face as I raise my hand as if to capture the wind. A tornado forms in my palm. Dax takes a few steps back.

"Addie . . . what are you going to do?"

I open my mouth and blow the small tornado toward the prisoner. He twists his body and yells as it lengthens in size, lifting him up off the ground. I blow harder and the prisoner spirals back against the wall. With a wave of my hand, the tornado dissipates, but I leave the prisoner pinned up against an emergency fire hydrant inside of a glass case.

"Addison? What are you going to do to him?" I ignore the concern in my brother's voice and lift a finger to my mouth, moving closer to the prisoner.

"Shhh . . . I'm not going to hurt you." The prisoner's eyes are wide, his pupils shaking as the everlasting blood from his spikes of torture trickles down his chest. "I don't know what you did, nor do I know how long you've been like this. Whether you deserve it or don't. But either way, you can't stay like this forever." I wave my arms halfway toward my face and vines materialize from the walls. His eyes move frantically from side to side, unable to move, panicked. The vines grip onto the cage kissing his head. With one more flick of my wrist, the vines yank on the metal and break the prisoner free. Metal from the broken cage clashes the floor one last and final time.

He coughs a few times and stretches his jaw and swallows.

"There, that feels better, doesn't it?"

The prisoner lifts his head up to breathe, but more coughs come out.

I reach into my coat pocket and pull out the crane bag. Holding it tightly in my hand, the prisoner winces. He relaxes as soon as he sees it's a small leathery pouch.

"If you come inside, I will make sure that you will no longer be tortured. Will you trust me?" The prisoner lowers his eyes, studying the bag for a second, and then me. He nods once. I slowly unravel it, cautious not to release the other spirits inside, but quick enough in case he gets any ideas and tries to escape. The prisoner's physical body starts to become translucent. His head, now in the form of a ghost, elongates and stretches, as he gets sucked into the bag. The rest of his body follows and I close him in.

I attach the crane bag back to my belt loop when a tantalizing pain strikes my temples. I fall to my knees and grip my forehead.

"Addison? What's the matter?" Dax runs to my side.

"Oh, it hurts!"

"What hurts? Show me!"

"My head!" My breathing quickens, and tears roll down my face. "What's happening?"

"Let me see, Addison." Dax grabs my hands and forces them from my face. My eyes are shut as I force back tears. I finally give in and let him peel my hands away. Dax gasps.

"What is it?" I cry.

"Addison, your face . . . your eyes . . . and horns."

"My what!?" I open my eyes and wipe my face.

"You summoned the last element."

"So, this means my horns are back?" I rub the top of my head, two twisted, short, but undoubtedly horns poke out.

"It doesn't look like they're fully out yet though."

"My head hurts, but it's feeling better." I get up off the floor and dust myself off. "What does this mean?"

Dax wrinkles his forehead and shakes his head, but the expression in his eyes tells me he doesn't think it's anything good.

Down the hall, Skadi whimpers as she hits a wall. I nearly choke on air and dodge out of the room. Eyes wide, I sprint to the hospital room where I had seen a demon hovering on top of one of the beds. I hope it's not too late.

"Not yours, you wretched creature," the demon says to Skadi, who has picked herself up, aiming to eat another soul.

"Stop right there." I enter with my chin raised high. I might not know if I've come to the limits of my power, or if this means I'm a full demon. But I have horns, damnit; I'm going to play the part.

The demon glares over his shoulder at us. Two white eyes protrude from its black translucent form. The room is large with several sick bodies in the beds, separated by blue moveable walls.

"You're too late," the demon hisses. "You should have gotten here sooner, instead of playing with that prisoner down the hall."

"Looks like I'm not too late to save the boy. Back away from him."

"And what are you going to do? Your horns aren't even fully out."

"I'm stronger than you think." I raise my hands and conjure up the energy I know will get the job done. The demon laughs and turns back toward the sick boy. He begins to suck out the boy's soul, lifting his little body. I unleash my rage and push my hands forward, sending out a wave of energy. I throw the dark demon off its course and send it crashing against the wall.

The demon expands, sending out an energy field and blocking out my magick.

That's a curveball I was not expecting! "Nooo!" I lunge forward to grab the kid, but I'm too late. The demon sucks in what's left of the boy's spirit.

"You failed," the demon says as he raises himself toward the ceiling.

"Where are they?" I yell. "What have you done with all the spirits from this hospital?"

"Ha. You think I answer to you? Little Miss Horns."

Unnerved by his mocking me, I remember when Azazel had been able to immobilize someone with a flick of his wrist. This entire time, I had been repeating the same process to muster the energy to perform my new magickal abilities. I focus again and repeat to myself; *immobilize.*

"They sustain me." The demon squints.

I take a single step forward, my voice low. "You lie. Who do you work for?"

"I work for no one! What have you done?" The demon squirms in his spot. A gleam of pride sparks in my chest as I manage to lift him into the air.

"Also a lie. You made a deal with someone, and I'm going to find out who."

"Release me, at once!"

"Who do you work for?" I bring out the crane bag. Skadi licks her lips, approaching me with caution. I grab on to her in the other hand. "What will it be? Do you want to be puppy chow before or after I open up my little bag and steal back all those spirits you've taken?" The demon broods, rendered speechless.

"What's wrong? Hellhound caught your tongue?" I start to unravel my bag-

"Wait! I'll make a deal with you."

I lower the bag. "Go on . . ."

"Addison?" Dax's concerned voice echoes through the room at my annoyance. I put a hand out to shush him.

"Let me go, and I'll tell you who's collecting souls."

"Tell me first, then I'll let you go."

The demon stays quiet for a moment. I shrug and start to unravel the bag.

"Wait, how do I know you'll release me?"

I fold my arms. "You don't. But it's your only choice."

"I don't know his name. But I know it's one of them." The demon moves his eyes toward Dax who screws up his face.

"What the hell does that mean?"

"A reaper."

I purse my lips together and my nostrils flare. "You think I'm a fool? Keep lying to me, see where that gets you!" I push the crane bag toward the demon.

"No, no! I'm telling the truth. It's a reaper. A reaper has been collecting souls. He promised us a new hierarchy in his new world, a better life!"

I drop my hand. "New world? What do you mean? What does a reaper need new souls for?"

"He's creating an army," he spits.

I scrunch my nose up, unsure if he's telling the truth. I glance at Dax, whose face is also just as screwed up as mine.

"What does a reaper want with an army?" Dax asks.

"A takeover," I mutter, responding for the demon.

"There, I told you what you wanted, now let me go."

I curl my lips. "So that you could go running back to your boss? I don't think so."

"No, I won't. He'll kill me!"

"Not my problem." I open the crane bag. Like a magnet, it sucks in all of the spirits the demon had stolen from the sick and dying in the hospital. A bright, glowing river of souls streams inside, like a waterfall. When the last drip of souls falls in, I tie it back together and hook it onto my belt loop.

"Now that you have your spirits, let me go."

"That's no way to talk to your new Queen." I chide with a hint of sarcasm in my voice, turning to Skadi who's sitting patiently by my leg, waiting for her master to finish. She starts slapping the tile floor with her tail.

"Who's a good girl? Are you hungry?"

"What?" The demon shrieks. "No, we had a deal! We had a deal!"

"This is for my coworkers!" I pat Skadi on her back. "Dinner!" The hellhound jumps through the air and chomps down on the demon's face first. The demon screams and shrieks, but in two gulps, he's gone, never to be heard again. Skadi licks her lips.

"Good girl."

The swooshing sounds of a portal opens up behind me, low vents opening causing wind to pass through my hair. I turn to face a tall skeletal man beneath a hooded cloak, bearing a scythe. As he steps onto the hospital floor, my stomach churns as his dark sunken eyes peer deep into my soul. I swallow hard. *Ambrose, could that be you?* The man drops his cloak and his eyes begin to fill, his facial structure starts to change. He has white hair and a pointy nose. Two more reapers step out of a portal behind him right before the portal closes.

Dax charges toward me, shielding me with his arm.

"There you are, Dax. Not doing your job, I see."

Not doing his job? "What does he mean, Dax?" I stop his arm from pushing me back further.

"Leave her alone, Lorcan. You know very well I was recruited for a different duty."

"Hogwash, we don't take orders from Deacon, Dax, you know that. Addison, I believe you have something of mine."

But they do take orders from Deacon . . . I quirk a brow at him. "Oh? What's that?"

Lorcan points at my cloak with a raised eyebrow. "Hand it over, please. Don't make me take it from you."

"I have no idea what you're talking about. And what do you mean you don't take orders from Deacon? I thought she was the new Judge."

"Oh, is that what they've been telling you? More lies?" Lorcan strides slowly toward me. Dax pushes me behind him and stands in front of Lorcan.

"Dax? What's going on?"

Lorcan tuts his tongue on the roof of his mouth five times, shaking his head slowly. "Your crane bag, Addison."

"*My crane bag?*" I place my hand on it. "Um, no. You're not getting this. This doesn't belong to you."

"That's where you're wrong. What's inside of it is indeed mine," Lorcan snaps.

My jaw drops. "You're the reaper who's been having demons collect souls for you . . ."

"Fast one, isn't she?" Lorcan says. A chuckle rises from one of the two reapers who haven't moved since they got here.

"But, why?" I mutter.

"Because LLAPS needs a reboot. And its new current"—Lorcan clears his throat—"administration is an abomination at best. The Reaper Council is flawed by human emotion, which isn't the way of the reapers."

Dax raises his voice. "Oh, and using the demons to form an army is the right way?"

"We need to be ruling LLAPS, Dax, not the demons. Not some king or queen of demons. Us. The rule-makers, the ones who know how to keep order. Us, Dax. And certainly not your sister."

"The new judge has been doing a great job so far. He's been picking up the pieces from the mess Azazel left, and instead of you helping, you've been conspiring against him. You wouldn't make a good ruler, Lorcan, sorry to say."

I screw up my face, my eyebrows knit together as I glance at the floor for a second. "He? I thought you said the new judge was Deacon . . ." My eyes squint at my brother. "Dax?"

"Actually, Dax, you do make a fine point. There is something the new Judge did I completely agree with."

"Oh yeah? And what's that?"

"He put an APB on all demons. I was going to take care of the ones I had sent to do my bidding after they'd finished, of course."

Dax extends his arm out once again to protect me.

"You can't protect her, Dax. This is exactly what I'm talking about. You're a reaper. You can't be letting your emotions get in the way of your reaping." Lorcan paces back and forth, shaking his head.

"Dax, what the hell is he talking about?"

"You should tell her, Dax, or should I?"

Dax's eyebrows arch as he hesitates to speak. His breathing shallows and I back away from him. "Dax? What are you not telling me?"

"Allow me. You see, Addison—"

"No, I'll tell her. Addie, the reason why I've been here with you instead of reaping souls and helping LLAPS is because Deacon told me I should help you."

I nod. "Yes, I know. You told me in the boat that reapers were after all demons. And that it was best for me to stay away and to help me save the prisoners that escaped from the guardsmen and revitalizers of LLAPS . . ."

"Well, that last part was all you but . . . there's more . . ."

"More?"

Dax nods. "You have to understand . . . I lied to keep you from jumping planes . . . You would have gotten killed . . ."

"Okay, but one thing I don't understand is, why couldn't someone just tell Deacon not to put an APB on all demons, or at least exclude me?"

Lorcan wipes his face. "Haven't you been listening? Deacon is not the new Judge. Your brother lied to you."

"Wait—What? Then who is?"

"Well, Ambrose of course," Lorcan says with a smug look on his face.

My face drops and my throat becomes dry. "What?"

"Addison, I can explain," Dax says. I look at him, waiting for an explanation. Dax gulps. "Deacon felt it was best to let Ambrose focus on being Judge."

"He put an order out to kill you, Addison. He saw what you became and couldn't stand the sight of you," Lorcan spits.

"Shut up, Lorcan. Addison, that isn't true. Don't listen to him." My heart sinks down to my stomach. Ambrose is the new Judge? So, he wasn't being kept busy . . .

"I don't have time for this." Lorcan turns toward the two reapers standing like statues, waiting for his command. "Seize her and bring me the crane bag."

I jump back as both reapers close in on me. One of

them, in full skeletal form, pushes me back and holds me up against the wall, as the other one searches for the crane bag. Raising my legs, I kick full force into the reaper's rib cage. I scramble my thoughts to muster some energy but can't focus while fighting them off. Lorcan takes out his scythe and presses it against my neck, causing my skin to sizzle. I wince, my breath shallow.

Dax reaches into his coat pocket and takes out his scythe. He raises it above his head and swings down on Lorcan. Lorcan spins around and clashes his scythe against Dax's, a bright blue light emanating from the blades hitting against each other.

ADDISON

My focus snaps to the reaper trying to pry my crane bag from my belt loop. I uppercut him in the skull.

Skadi jumps over from the woodworks and bites him from behind. The reaper takes out a pocket scythe, its blue light emerging and sending Skadi crashing through one of the blue hospital separators.

"No! Skadi!" The reaper grabs onto the crane bag, yanking it from my belt. I snap my hand down, hitting his bones. One reaper grabs my neck and pushes me back against the wall while the other reaper snaps the bag right off. Shit. I muster my energy as fast as I can and materialize vines out of the walls and ceilings—my apparent go-to at this stage. A vine swings from the side and grabs onto the crane bag, while two more vines seize both reapers.

I dust myself off, stretch my neck, and walk to the vine keeping my crane bag safe. I pick it up and turn to face Dax and Lorcan battling in hand-to-hand combat. Lorcan lets out an angry wail. With a fierce move of his arm, he blows Dax's scythe out of his grip, disarming him. Dax watches as his scythe clangs to the ground, he reaches for it, but Lorcan kicks him hard in the jaw. Dax falls face down on the floor with a thud and Lorcan turns his attention to me.

"Dax!" I run toward my brother, but I get intercepted by Lorcan. With a wave of his scythe, he releases the two reapers I had imprisoned with magick.

"This is exactly why I hate demons. Abuse of magick." Lorcan tuts. "With you out of my way, I'll succeed much faster. Ambrose will know you're dead, and it will be his fault."

"I thought you said he couldn't stand the sight of me."

"Lying to you is so easy, Addison."

My cheeks burn red.

Lorcan raises his scythe to my chin, forcing my face up. "I'll make this quick."

My breath grows heavy. The cold, sharp blade burns against my skin, but I keep my gaze fixed on Lorcan.

A flash of red surges behind Lorcan and burning heat from fire grazes my skin. A smile pastes on my face and Lorcan stops to look over his shoulder and gasps. Dax had gotten up and become full-on cloaked and skeletal. His hollow sockets burn with fire, and he throws a flame at Lorcan. Lorcan moves out of the way and it misses me by an inch as I dart sideways.

"What is this? How are you doing this?"

Dax jolts both arms, full of flames, to his sides, readying himself to aim them at Lorcan. Lorcan turns to me. "Killing you will be the best thing I do as leader. Getting rid of Lucifer's leavings. Best watch for your friends, Addison. I'll be seeing you again."

My eyes narrow. Threatening my friends, prick?

"Ava, is it?" Lorcan smiles.

One of the reapers opens a portal. Lorcan grabs my crane bag from my hand.

"No!"

Lorcan jumps through the portal, and it quickly closes behind him.

"Dax, you have to go after them!"

Dax returns to normal. "Sorry, Addie, I'm still getting the hang of that. Did you see Lorcan's face when he saw what I could do though?"

"He took it . . . Dax, he took the crane bag full of spirits." My voice croaks as I spot Skadi lying on the ground. I run to her and place my hand on the hellhound's big head, lifting it onto my lap. Skadi starts to wag her tail slowly.

Dax crouches down next to us. "She's just hurt." He places his scythe on top of Skadi, and it glows once, just like it did the time Ambrose brought back Crowley. Skadi gets up and licks Dax on the face.

"Good as new," Dax says, grimacing at the slobber.

I turn away, closing my eyes, focusing on my energy to retrieve the pouch. Holding out my hand, I expect the item to materialize in my palm. Heat rises but gets swooshed away. I try again.

"Addie, if you're doing what I think you're doing, I don't think it'll be of any use . . ."

"Why not? I know I can manifest it back."

"No, a scythe's power would be able to guard it against any demon. Against you."

My face rigid, I get up off the floor, avoiding Dax's gaze. The hospital is a disaster, and everyone is dead. I start to walk out of the room.

"Addison? Where are you going? We'll get it back . . ."

I turn to look at him. "No, *we* won't."

"What?"

"*I* will. You lied to me."

"Addison, I did it to protect you."

"*Protect me*? Protect me how? How is not telling me the truth protecting me, Dax?"

"I didn't want you to think Ambrose hated you. He doesn't even know you're—"

"A demon? Or part demon? Or whatever the hell I am? Do you think keeping this from him is even a good idea? He has reapers and guards trying to kill me, and he doesn't even know it!"

"I know, it's wrong. I agree with you. Deacon thought it best for him to focus on being Judge. With you on his mind, Addison, he wouldn't be able to . . ."

"You should have trusted me. You didn't need to lie."

Dax falls silent. "I know, I'm sorry. Deacon didn't want you to contact him. I wanted to tell you; I promise."

"Well, you chose a promise you made to Deacon over your own sister." I spin on my heel and walk out the door.

"Wait, where are you going?"

"To protect Ava."

"No, Addie, you can't go there. The reason why the LLAPS skies have been moving slowly is because they're following you. If you go to Miami, you'll take all of LLAPS with you."

I open my mouth to speak but realize he's right.

"Besides, this is exactly what Lorcan wants. For you to go save Ava so he can kill you. And he'll kill her anyway. He doesn't care about a human."

"I still have to try. Don't follow me."

BURY MY HEART

AMBROSE

*R*age thrums through me as I stand in a pile of two hundred hound demon corpses. Brave, dark souls; they're victims as much as we were, placed here to ambush Deacon and me. But no match for the golden scythe. Never a match. A regular scythe, no doubt, but not this beast of a thing. Undeniably though, a few were reapers among them. They fled as soon as they saw I'm not as weak as they assumed I was.

Grief-stricken, I stand, watching from the bridge of this trans-dimensional plane, at *her*. I had never known happiness until I met her. Until I gave myself to her. And now, not only can I not be with her, but I've failed her. My Addison. I should have been here to protect her.

I catch a reflection of her amber eyes as she passes me by, not being able to see me through the veil, and walks out the hospital door. A hint of her tropical shampoo brushes against my nostrils as she leaves and I take a moment to breathe her in.

"Let her go, Ambrose."

"She could have been killed, Deacon. This was wrong.

All of this was wrong. I should have told her I was alive, I should have at least come to her to tell her . . . goodbye."

"She would be too stubborn to let you go. I'm sorry I didn't tell you what she became." And this. Her horns on her head, her new powers. Could it have been suppressed? *Should* it have been suppressed? The fact that Azazel had his clutches on her makes my innards burn with rage. But as always, I keep a cool head.

"It's time." I open the portal and we both step onto the hospital room floor to a brooding Dax, still staring at the door, alone.

"Back for more?"

"You can relax, Dax, it's only us," Deacon says as we step down from the portal.

"Took you long enough."

"Yes, we saw everything," Deacon starts. "Lorcan had two hundred demons ambush us to keep us out." Deacon steps over some broken debris. I glance at Dax as he looks at me and heads over.

"Ambrose? It's so good to see you."

I nod. "And you." He lets go of the embrace and looks deeply into my skeletal eye sockets. "Not changing form?"

"I prefer to remain composed." It's best he doesn't see my features, hurt as I am.

"I understand. So, you tried to get here, but were stopped by Lorcan's buddies, huh?"

"Yes, it appears he has quite a few allies."

"He came here looking for Addison. He tried to kill her, Deacon."

"Because of the APB I put on her," I say.

"This wasn't your fault though," he says, turning to Deacon. "It's yours."

Deacon tilts her head back. "Mine?"

"Yes, because of you, reapers took it upon themselves to try and kill my sister. We've been hiding from revitalizers, guardsmen, all while Addison has been trying to do the right thing and save the damn prisoners." My stomach knots. Of course, she has. She might have demon blood in her, but there isn't an evil bone in her body.

"I've been trying to keep her from turning into a full-on demon, and now she won't even talk to me, because I lied to her. Because you asked me to lie to her." Dax points a rigid finger to her chest and it accidentally ignites. His eyes meet mine and then Deacon's.

"Dax, you need to relax," I say. "Deacon was doing what she thought was necessary."

His jaw drops. Of course it does. He wants to protect his sister, and I don't blame him. I do too. Hell, I'd be pissed at Deacon too if I didn't know what was at stake here. I know why she did it, and although I don't agree with her method, I know how Deacon's mind works. Always for the good of the council, and she's scrambling to keep things right. The last thing she needs is a reaper-demon love drama.

"You're siding with her? But she lied to you too!"

"Believe me, I was shocked to find out Addison is a demon. You have no idea how much it pains me. But Azazel had been right. She had it in her. And if this is who she is—what needed to come out—I will love her either way. I will always love her, Dax. Rest assured, I will mend the APB, to exclude Addison in the killing of all demons. But, that won't stop Lorcan now."

"Correct, now that we know what he's up to, he's considered rogue." Deacon says.

"What do I do about Addison? She doesn't want me to follow her."

"Don't. Addison can take care of herself. We have bigger

problems. Like me, Dax, you have to accept the bigger responsibility of what comes with being a reaper. A responsibility greater than saving your sister."

Dax lets out a soft, shallow breath of air, hearing those words come out of my mouth. If only he knew how much it pained me as well. How much I want to reach out to her. Hold her in my arms. Keep her from harm, above all else. But how can I tell him I was never able to keep her safe? Because I was as much a fool to fall victim to Azazel's powers. Allowed myself to get captured. Killed. It was embarrassing.

"I can't believe you. I thought you said you still love her."

"And I do, but we need to trust that she can handle herself. Right now, we need you to come with us. Lorcan has convinced many of the council members he'd make a better ruler, despite what the Akashic waters said. If we run to Addison's aid, Lorcan will know his baiting me is working. He intends to kill me for the power over the scythe."

"He can do that to become Judge? What about the waters?"

"The only way he can kill me might be by another one of Azazel's weapons, being the dagger Addison lost. You wouldn't happen to know where it is?"

"Oh, fuck me. Yes, Addie has it. She manifested it back to herself. We need to go back to her, Ambrose."

"It's too dangerous. As long as she doesn't use it in front of him, he might not know she has it. But if we go to her, we'll be making it easy for Lorcan to pit his army against us, more importantly, against her. It'll be too difficult to keep her safe that way. Come with us. We have a plan."

Dax nods. "Makes sense."

From what I saw, Addie won't need to use it anyway.

"With most of the reapers on his side, and this scythe, a new legion army of prisoners, new souls, and demons, he'll be able to do what he pleases."

Deacon places her hand on Dax's shoulder. "Expect a war, Dax. And we need your help to prepare."

I AM MY OWN PROTECTOR

ADDISON

Ambrose is the new Judge of the Reaper Council. How the hell did that happen? How could Dax keep such a secret from me? This entire time Ambrose didn't know I was a demon either? I shake my head. Still though. He could have come to see me. Screw being Judge and screw the council. He still could have come . . .

Fog escapes my lips as I leave the hospital, the dead, cold air of LLAPS slowing down my step. Reminding me of the dire issue at hand. Skadi, mesmerized by the rustling of leaves in a nearby bush, crouches down as she walks, sniffing the ground. The sky is a dark purple, signifying the portals dropping out LLAPS's guardsmen have completely joined the two worlds. Or, as it stands, wherever I go.

"Come on, Skadi. Let's go. We don't need Dax's help." Saying it out loud doesn't make it true. A sinking feeling in my gut tells me I need to get to Ava, but I'd be open to anything and everything that wants to kill me without my brother's protection.

"I don't need him." Skadi looks up at the sound of my voice. I look back at the hospital, half waiting for him to come out. A flash of rage sweeps through me. *Still can't believe he lied.* "Skadi, what are you doing? Come on, girl." I jog over to the bush to pull Skadi away when a low moaning makes me crouch down by the bush Skadi is so intently looking at. A ghostly head floats low to the ground, terrified at the enormous hellhound wanting to eat it.

I lean on into Skadi, attempting to push her away despite her purposely weighing herself down like a pile of bricks. "Move over, Skadi. That isn't your food."

Skadi licks her lips.

"I said, no." I push her even harder. Skadi growls but doesn't budge. I turn to the floating head. "I'm sorry, Lorcan stole my crane bag. Without it, I can't save you." The floating head moans. "Can you try to go back to LLAPS? The astral has seeped through to this plane, there must be a way back for you somehow." The head moans back, its eyes sullen and harrowing. "Can you even understand me?" The head doesn't respond. I sigh. Skadi whimpers and her stomach growls loud enough for me to hear. I place a hand on the pup's head to scratch it. "You're always hungry, aren't you? I'll gather up some egregores for you back at the house."   I open my cloak pocket and pull out Rezmelda's pouch.

Not sure if this is an actual crane bag, *per se*, but it does the same thing . . . Could it transport actual human spirits though, spirits with thoughts, instead of mindless egregores? "If I put you in here, promise you won't try to escape? Not sure if this bag can hold you." The head floats upward, toward my face. Skadi gets up, wagging her tail. "Be still, you. This isn't for you."

I open up the empty bag, and the floating head willingly goes in it. The bag doesn't suck it in like the crane bag would have, but this would have to do for now. Maybe I can still save a few after all.

"Ready, Skadi? Let's go home. We're not going to get to Miami on foot." Skadi growls. "Yes, I promise I'll pick up your snacks."

There's no difference between the cold temperature outside and the temperature inside of the mansion. The first thing I do is walk to the library to check on my dad. I place my hand on his neck but he looks alright. He's breathing and peacefully sleeping. I drape a blanket over him as the house has gotten colder since the last time I had been here. "Wherever you are, dad, I hope you come back soon." I walk over to the hidden passageway to the astral plane, behind the bookcase. Taking hold of Rezmelda's bag, I look down at Skadi. "Get back, Skadi. Do not go running in. I'm only letting this little guy go so I can put your food in. Can't have egregores and spirits in the same bag. It'll be too confusing." Skadi tilts her head as if trying to understand me. I hold on to the hidden lever by her dad's grimoire and take a deep breath. Once I open this door, anything can come out of it from the other side. Guardsmen could be waiting for me, a revitalizer could come in, or Lorcan could have reapers standing outside of it. *This is risky.* But what other choice do I have? I can't take this spirit with me. I tug on the lever and walk swiftly toward the door while opening up the pouch. The head floats out and looks at me.

"Go on, through that door. Keep floating all the way and you'll make it back to LLAPS."

The floating head moans.

"I know, this isn't ideal, but I can't take you with me. You have to hurry, there isn't much time. We can't let anyone know about this portal. Go!" The floating head widens its eyes as it moves backward through the air, giving me a look of despair as I shut the door. I hope it'll be alright. I just let it go back to the place it was trying to escape from. I shake my head. But at the same time, there's no difference between here or there right now. I will go back for them.

I tap on the side of my cloak, where my dagger is. "I haven't needed this lately to perform spells. I think I'm lucky Lorcan didn't take this from me too. Maybe he was too focused on stealing the spirits and didn't see it. With this, as Azazel declared, all demons can be commanded. In the wrong hands, that would be catastrophic. Not sure if keeping it on me is safest, but if I leave it here with my dad, it could attract harm to him." I leave it tucked in. The house is warded, better to not attract anything that could try to disarm it.

Skadi whimpers by my legs. "Right, now it's your turn."

Searching within, I visualize what an egregore normally looks like. The ugly little garden gnome with fangs that appears whenever I'm scared, or the little mushrooms that had fallen out of Rezmelda's pouch. No matter what emotions they evoke, Skadi will eat them.

I open up the pouch and hold my hand out to emanate a different emotion, one at a time, beginning with anger, since it's my most recent sentiment. Followed by betrayal, for my brother's secrecy, and then fear, for the potential threat of what's to come. A tiny silvery reaper mimicking Lorcan slithers out from the tips of my fingers and hops inside. A few more glide in and I turn toward Skadi who, for a hellhound, is being the most patient I've seen her be.

"Good girl, Skadi; maybe you are trainable." I focus on my memories one more time, allowing Skadi to have her fill before leaving. A few representations of the loss of love come out as a broken heart, a moon, and a scythe. Skadi licks them all in one gulp.

One more spell and we're done. I shut my eyes and focus on a dark mass of energy at the top of my head. No one will ever get to deceive me, ever again. Not my family, not a lover, not anyone. The black mass drops down on me, covering my head, down to my shoulders, and all the way down to my feet. Until I'm in a cocoon of dark energy. Protected from deception once and for all.

"Come on, we have a long drive ahead of us." Leaving the library, I pass the mirror I had turned to ice. Most of it has melted and my own reflection makes me look closer. The semblance of two horns trying to protrude out of my head makes tears swell up in my eyes. *Look what I've become. How am I going to show my face to Padrino like this?*

I walk to my bedroom and open my dresser drawer, looking for a hat or something to cover my horns with. I find a few headbands in an assortment of colors. Remembering what Padrino had told me once before about colors—dark colors attract evil spirits—I choose the white headband and put it on, then cover my head further with the hood of my cloak.

RESCUE MISSION

ADDISON

Well, I guess I can't drive off without warding my car too. Last thing I need is to have a high-speed chase with revitalizers on my tail. And cops, when I get to Miami. Focusing on the hood of my car, I visualize a blanket of power lifting from the ground, encasing every corner of my blue Volkswagen beetle. A shimmer of magick lifts from the car and I lower my hands.

With Skadi in the back seat, taking up all the space, even with the seats lowered to the trunk, it's a tight fit. At first, I adhere to the speed limit for a residential neighborhood, but as soon as I hit the road, I book it. Normally, it would take an hour and a half to get from Tavernier Key to Miami, but without any traffic, I'd like to make it there in forty.

I put my phone on speaker and call Ava.

"Oh my God, Addison, I've been worried sick."

"How's it looking over there?"

"Still the same, fewer people on the roads but Padrino told me to stay in the house, so I don't know."

"Good, are you all at the house, then?"

"Yeah, we're all here, why?"

"I'm on my way."

"You are? What's going on?"

"You'll see when I get there. Tell Padrino to protect the house with a warding spell. I think you guys will freak when you see me."

"The house always has a protection spell on it. Why will we freak?"

"I just . . . look different. But Ava, whatever you do, do not go outside. Not sure your grandpa's warding spells will do anything. I'll be there as soon as I can."

"Are we warding against demons?"

"Not exactly . . ."

"I *definitely* don't like the sound of this."

"See you soon." I hang up the phone and push down on the accelerator.

I race toward blue skies up the highway, out of the Florida Keys. In my rear-view mirror, purple skies follow my path. Skadi lies in the backseat with her head resting on the door frame. She snaps out the window as a guardsman appears, swinging his ax above his head. I swerve the car and hit the accelerator. "Hold on, Skadi."

The rest of the way, I don't bother stopping to check on any spirits or to save any people. Powers or not, I'm one person, and saving Ava is my highest priority.

The sky is still blue as I reach a red light, finally at Miami. LLAPS hasn't reached here yet—but why aren't there any cars? Ava's right. Things do seem different. Was this how the Keys was before LLAPS completely took over? So, it wasn't a fast takeover. There must be demons nearby collecting souls.

As I pull up to Ava's house, their front door swings open. Ava runs outside, ready to wrap her arms around me. Her face drops though as soon as she sees what's in the back seat.

"Addison, what the hell is that? Is that a *dog*?"

I ignore the question. "Ava, what are you doing out here? I told you to stay inside!"

"Yeah, but it's okay, for a second."

"No, let's get inside."

Padrino steps outside as well.

"Is no one listening to me? We need to get inside." Padrino opens his mouth to speak but gasps when he sees Skadi inside of the car.

"How did you—how is that—? Addison, that cannot come inside."

"I'm sorry, it's a long story, but she's friendly. I couldn't leave her."

Ava peers through the car window. "Holy shit, are its eyes red? It's huge!"

"It's a hellhound."

Ava's eyes widen. "A what? What the hell, Addison?"

"Come with me," Padrino says. "Bring your hellhound around to the back. We'll leave her in the back room, where she can't eat any of the spirits we welcome in this house."

I let out a sigh. "I'm sorry, I forgot about that." I open the car and let Skadi out.

"Does she have a name?" Ava asks.

"I named her Skadi after the Norse goddess of hunting and damage."

"Good name. What does she eat?" Ava opens up the gate and leads us to the back room through the yard.

"Literally anything you give her. She's come a long way though. I have her on a strict egregore diet."

"How did you manage that?"

I take out the pouch and let out an egregore into the

back shed we're going to keep Skadi in. A little reaper hops out and Skadi flies over our shoulders and takes it in one gulp. I let out a few more egregores and shut the door.

Ava's mouth hangs open.

"I made them from emotions."

Ava closes her mouth. "Okay, yeah, we have a lot to talk about. Let's get inside."

Padrino steps in next to me. "That was very clever, but I do not think that will hold her hunger for very long. They eat real spirits."

I hadn't considered if it would be enough or not. "I can't just let her eat spirits though."

"There is a circle of life, Addison. You know that. Even for creatures of other realms. Come on, Madrina is making us some coffee inside."

The idea of entering a normal household and drinking coffee around a kitchen table calms my nerves.

"So, what did you mean by you look different? You look the same to me," Ava says as she clears the kitchen table and sits down. I lower the hood of my cloak and take off my headband. Ava covers her mouth with her hand. "Grandpa? Come here!"

Madrina walks in and sets down four espresso cups. She does a double-take at my head. "Oh, girl, you did it this time, didn't you?" She shakes her head.

"This isn't even important. Ava, I came here to protect you. You're all in danger."

Madrina sits down across from me. "What do you mean we're all in danger? What's going on?"

I take a deep breath and place my hands on the table.

"What is happening in here? Why is everybody shouting?" Padrino asks, walking in carrying a few glasses of water. I turn toward him, pulling my hair back so my horns are visible. Padrino's eyes grow wide, with one arched eyebrow, but he doesn't say anything. He scrunches his forehead and pulls up a chair next to me. He clears his throat, and then takes a sip of his coffee, closing his eyes to savor it. "Ya, *calmate*. Relax, Addison. Drink your coffee and we will talk."

I've always felt like I could be myself around Padrino. No matter the circumstance, I never have to hide. I pick up my espresso cup and take a sip, letting the familiar aromas of my culture soothe me. A reminder of something constant, and hope by being here, everything will get figured out.

Padrino sets his cup down. "It looks to me like you are still searching for who you are. After all this time."

This again? "I don't understand . . ."

"Why do you think your horns aren't out fully? They look as if they want to come out, but you don't let them."

I screw up my face. "No, I don't want them to come out. How is this normal to you?"

"What's normal to the spider is chaos for the fly," he says. "Whatever happened to you when you went to the other side clearly changed you, but it didn't change who you are inside, only physically."

I nod, remembering how I found out about my demon blood and having to reach my full potential. "So I've been told. But when I came back, I didn't look like this. I looked normal. I don't want to look like this." I flick my gaze frantically from Ava to Padrino.

"Yes, well, that is another story. I see what is going on outside, it seems like you brought that world with you. That power is causing things to change here, which is why you can change your form so easily. Your magick is also different, isn't it?"

I glance across the kitchen to the family room window.

The sky is beginning to become purple. We're running out of time. I nod.

"Only you can change yourself back. But first, you need to accept what you are."

"I thought you wouldn't approve of me being a demon. You know . . . evil."

Padrino laughs.

I raise an eyebrow and glance at Ava, who rolls her eyes once and looks back down at her cup. "What's so funny?"

"Angels, demons, up, down, what's the difference? Besides the way we use our power!"

I reach for my glass of water. "But when I tried to use my magick when I first became like this, it messed up my spells."

"Let me ask you a question." Padrino moves in closer. "Do you want to be like this? What you call it? A demon?"

"No . . . not really, I didn't have much of a choice—"

"Stop. Do you not like your power?"

"Well, yes, that I do."

"So, you do want to be like this."

"No! Not exactly . . ."

"That's the problem."

I slam down my glass of water, causing it to freeze over. Ava and Madrina's eyes widen and they sit back from the table.

"I'm sorry . . . but, you see?"

"Do not worry, mi niña. Ice melts. But this is my point. Your inner conflict is what's messing with your magick. Your mixed feelings are sending mixed signals. Do you understand?"

"But I wasn't able to channel anything by focusing on happiness."

Padrino shakes his head. "Of course not. It is easier for

you to feel angry than truly happy. You cannot fake happiness and mean it inside of you. But anger? Not much faking has to be done."

I shrug one shoulder and nod a few times. "So, then, what do I do?"

"First, you must accept your changes."

"Okay, I can try."

"And then, you need to place your powers in a neutral chamber of your emotions."

"I don't follow."

"Let me show you."

Padrino takes his glass of water. "This glass of water represents who you were before these dark powers." He hands the glass back to me. "Now, pour the rest of your coffee into the glass."

I chuckle. "Really?"

"Yes, do it."

I do as I'm told. The warm coffee turns the water black from the top and slowly makes its way down.

"Is all of the water mixed with coffee?"

"Yes."

"Yes? Then why is the bottom of the glass still clear?"

"Well, it's getting there."

"But it hasn't completely reached the bottom yet."

"If I stir it, it will mix faster."

"Okay then, stir it with your finger, go on."

I squint at Padrino and he smiles. "You can wash your hands after; hurry up and do it." So much for a second of normalcy. I stir the coffee water in the glass. Ava laughs and hands me a napkin.

"Okay, now what?"

"Now, look at the water. What color is it?"

"It's like . . . brownish black from the coffee."

"Good, now separate the coffee from the water."

I curl my lips. "That's impossible. I can't."

"That's not true," says Madrina, who had been sitting idly watching.

Padrino sits back in his chair. "You see? You give up too easily."

"Well, how? Do you mean by magick?"

Padrino raises a brow. "Maybe. Is there not another way?"

My eyebrows knit together as I gaze down at the glass of dirty water. "I guess I could filter it."

"Aha!" Padrino sits up in his chair. "If you put the water through a filter, it may take some time and repeated sessions, but you can clean the water, yes. You are right."

"Oh, I get it." Ava takes hold of the water glass and looks into it. I grab it and slide the glass back toward me.

"Great, glad you do. But I still don't follow. What does this have to do with me? Are you going to filter out the black magick from my soul?" I get up from my seat and dump the glass of water in the sink.

Padrino bellows with laughter. "Like I said, you give up too easily."

My cheeks flush, but I hold my tongue. Padrino leans forward. "Magick is neutral, as we are when we are born. It passes through filters, and that is how it claims what it is, and what it does."

"There's one problem with this theory, Padrino. I have demon blood in me. I was destined to be the most powerful with dark magick. Worse than that, I already said before that when I tried to use my power how I used to, everything got mixed up."

"My dear, you still do not understand. It doesn't matter what blood you have in you, or if your spirit comes from a place with a lower vibration, or a higher vibration." He smiles as he stands up and touches my hands. "Angels, demons, humans, magical creatures, we are living things trying to make sense of this energy given to us. Energy is energy and giving it direction is magick. Find your neutral spot and bring it to a higher vibration. Or a lower one, if that is what you want."

My eyes light up and I lift my chin. "Alchemy," I whisper.

Padrino wrinkles his forehead. "What was that?"

"Alchemy! I understand what Azazel was telling me. Although he was trying to get me to give in to my darkness, I know now what he means by transcendence."

Padrino nods. "You have to find your balance and live in it. Your higher self isn't about heaven, or good memories, it's about accepting who you are and emerging your power from clean energy, not angry energy. That creates chaos. And not only happy memories or good energy; that creates unbalance. But by accepting who you are. Only then can your magick do anything."

I hug him tight. "Thank you."

"Anytime, mija."

I pull away and rub my head. "I don't want to be Queen of LLAPS, or hell as everyone here knows it. I can feel so much darkness coming from there and I'm afraid I'll lose myself."

"Wait," Ava says. We both look at her. "How does she know when she reaches her higher self? What does she have to do?"

"So far, my magick doesn't work like it used to, but I can use elemental magick. So long as I do the opposite of what I used to . . . I need to reach my neutral space." I glance at Padrino and give him a smile.

"So, you're like Avatar?"

"Like what? The movie?"

"No, like the TV series *Avatar*."

"Never seen it."

"Seriously? Have you been living under a rock?"

I stare at her blankly and she rolls her eyes.

"In *Avatar*, the characters master their elemental powers."

"Ah. Well, I'm not mastering it, more like unleashing it within me. Every time I unleash an element, something happens. It's like I'm going through some sort of demon-trial puberty or something." I chuckle. "You know, it's kind of funny though. This is a power usually meant for light magick witches, not demons. Here I am reaching into my darkness for it."

"According to Western culture at least," Ava adds.

"True."

Ava grabs the rest of the coffee cups and glasses and brings them into the kitchen. "What's it like in there anyway? Is it all fiery and full of demons with wings and stuff?"

"A bit, but mostly it's a prison, full of humans being tortured from their lives here on Earth."

"Wow, so it's true then . . . heaven, hell."

"No, not really. Everyone is trapped in their own torture. They can change it, but they don't know how because their freedom of consciousness was taken from them. Kind of like how we feel when we dream."

"So a prison then."

"Yes, but it's more than that. They can rise above their own torment because they're the ones causing it. LLAPS is a place to hold them. If they can somehow wake up, and learn from their mistakes, then perhaps they can rise above them and change."

"That is a good observation, Addison," Padrino says. "See, now you are thinking. And who can show them this?"

I shrug.

"Think about what *this* LLAPS means to *you*?"

I look off to the side. "Maybe it means giving people a second chance."

"And do you have to be an evil demon to do that?"

"No, I guess I don't." Loud barking comes from the back of the house and I jump. "Skadi!"

Ava turns to me and puts her hand on her chest. "I almost forgot about her. Addie, you said you came because we were in danger, or because *I* was in danger. Why?"

I sit back down. "This is kind of a long story. First of all, my brother lied to me. I thought Ambrose was dead at first, which he did tell me about, but Dax failed to mention he became the new Judge of the Reaper Council. Meaning, it's up to him to make the laws and protect the order of things. But instead, he sent guards out to kill me."

Ava's eyes widen.

"I thought Ambrose died when we were in LLAPS. My jaw tenses as I look down as I catch her up to the rest of the details. "Deacon came to Dax while I was sleeping to return his scythe, which he kept secret until I guess he couldn't anymore. That's when he told me Ambrose was alive but kept the fact he was the new Judge a secret. He knew he but didn't tell me."

"But why though?"

"Because Deacon told him to keep it a secret from me so that Ambrose would focus on being the new Judge. I guess they didn't tell him I turned into a demon and needed him to not worry."

"It sounds like your brother was following orders. He was in a tough spot, Addie."

"I don't care. He should have trusted me with the truth. That's not all. Not all the reapers are happy with Ambrose being the Judge. Which is probably the real reason Deacon wanted to keep us apart."

"Right, reapers and humans can't be together." Ava nods.

"Well, Deacon's little secret caused Ambrose to put an APB on all demons that escaped LLAPS. If you've looked outside, you can see LLAPS seeping through to this plane."

"Oh, so that's what's happening!"

I swallow hard. "Demons, prisoners, guardsmen are all here. It's crazy outside. And there are reapers after me. Lorcan has made it his personal mission to kill me and said he would go after my friends to get to me."

"Girl, and you came here?" Madrina stands up from her chair.

Padrino holds out his hand. "Calm down, Madrina. She came because she knew she had no other choice."

I turn to Madrina. "Lorcan will come anyway. He cornered me. If I didn't, he could come and kill you anyway to show me how serious he is. I don't know what this reaper is capable of, but I know it isn't empathy. He doesn't care about humans."

"Okay, so what do we do?" Ava asks.

"The wardings you put on the house will probably keep you safe against demons, but not reapers. For that, I'll have to be ready." A loud, ravenous growl comes from where Skadi is being kept, followed by furious barking and a loud bang. We run across the living room to the back room and open the door to find a giant hole through the wall of the shed. Skadi is gone.

A vent rumbles behind us, sending wind blowing through my hair. I crane my neck as three reapers step out from a portal.

"*L*orcan."

"I knew you'd be here. Just couldn't help your-self, could you, *Addison*?" I grimace at the way he spits my name like I'm some sort of poison he's trying to clear off his tongue as he emphasizes it, and a sinister smile grows on his face.

A glint of hope that it's Ambrose tightens my chest. Lorcan smiles and shakes his head as he sees the twinkle in my eye disappear. The portal releases several dark clouds.

"Ava, get back!" I yell, spreading my arm out to guard her against him. Madrina takes Ava by the arm and rushes down the hall toward one of the bedrooms. Lorcan tuts and stomps the dull end of his scythe on the ground.

Air catches in my throat as I follow the dark clouds out of the spinning void with my eyes. Lorcan spreads his arms, and the dark clouds swell in size, forming into the black, cloaked masses of revitalizers. They follow Madrina and Ava into the bedroom, while one stays to hover above Padrino.

"No, please let them go! They have nothing to do with

this! I'll do whatever you want! You want to kill me? Then fine, here I am!"

"No," Lorcan spits. "We will wait for your Ambrose to show up. Then he will watch as I kill you. Every minute he isn't here, I kill one of your friends."

My face tightens. "Why? Why are you doing this?"

"Because Ambrose thought he could be above it all. A relationship with a human. That's disgusting. He isn't fit to be Judge; I am!"

"It wasn't his choice, the Akashic waters chose him!"

"And I can change it. With the power from harvested souls, I can change the course of nature. Ambrose hasn't only consorted with a human, but a human with demon blood! That can only mean chaos for the astral plane. No, the moment I saw what you became I knew you'd have to be stopped. But the moment I saw the scythe choose Ambrose as my Judge, I knew the system was flawed and my mission became clear. You both need to die." I jump back as Lorcan hits his scythe against the floor and the portal closes.

A bright light emerges around Padrino, causing the revitalizer to shrink. Holy shit. I didn't think that was possible.

"Padrino!" I run to him just as he falls back against the wall and the revitalizer dissipates into thin air. She holds up his arm, helping him to his feet. His eyes look tired from summoning up so much energy. He looks up at me, urgency in his eyes, and points toward the hall. "Go, I'll take care of him."

"I—I don't know how to do what you did."

"Yes you do, Addison. Find your balance!"

The two reapers approach Padrino and grab him by his arms, bringing him up high to face Lorcan.

"Leave him alone!" I yell.

"Leave me, Addison. Go help them." Padrino tilts his

head toward me as he softens his eyes. I hesitate to turn around but do what he says. I run over to the bedrooms and find Ava and Madrina on the ground, gripping onto each other's arms as the revitalizers float above them. One of them looms toward me and I draw my hands together and close my eyes, searching for a neutral focus. This is making more sense. The revitalizers aren't good or evil, they're neutral. I need to do the same thing with my magick. Find my balance.

"Time is running out," Lorcan says. I bring up the most neutral object I can imagine, a piece of gold. A magnetic wave of energy pours through my hands. I open my eyes and the revitalizer had backed away from me and my friends. Now to get rid of them. *How did Padrino do that?*

"I'm getting bored, Addison." Lorcan's voice booms through the hall.

My blood curdles. "Madrina! Get up!" I shout. Madrina looks up at me and sees that the revitalizer has backed up. She lets go of Ava and faces it.

It isn't going anywhere. My heart pounds. I'm caught between saving Ava and her aunt or saving her grandfather. "I'm sorry . . . I have to help Padrino."

"Go!" Madrina shouts and holds hands with Ava. They close their eyes and murmur a few words. A flash of white light emanates from their bodies and blasts the revitalizers, shrinking them in size until they disappear.

"H–how?"

"Go, run!"

I turn on my heel and dash back toward Lorcan, who stands before his lackeys keeping Padrino prisoner.

Madrina freezes at the sight of them. I take slow strides as I approach Lorcan.

"Lorcan, I understand how you feel. This has all been

unfair to you. And you're right. Maybe the judge shouldn't be Ambrose. I for one never asked to be Queen of LLAPS, and I can see how you wouldn't want to allow that decision to be made by a demon, one like Azazel, no less."

Lorcan raises his brows. "I'm glad you see it my way, Addison. Maybe you're not as daft as I thought you were."

"So then, maybe we can work something out. Let Padrino go, please. I beg of you. He never did anything to deserve this."

"See, the problem still remains. Ambrose is Judge. And you have too much power. He won't give up the scythe. Not without your help."

"What am I supposed to do?"

"Call him here."

"Call him? How?"

Lorcan points at my neck. I look down and touch my necklace. "This? It doesn't work. I've tried to call him many times, but he never came. I thought he was dead."

"If he loves you, he'll sense you're in danger and come for you."

This whole time I've been in danger and this whole time he's been alive and never come for me. I shake my head. "He won't."

"Then say goodbye to one of your friends." He tilts his head toward Ava and one of his lackey reapers walks over to her.

"No!" I grab her arm but am pushed out of the way by the other reaper.

"Let her go!"

"Then call him."

"I don't know how!"

Suddenly, another portal opens up from the ceiling. A white horse with a rider wearing a red cape lands on the floor. The rider runs past and swings his sword, taking out both reapers in one go. My jaw drops. *Who the hell is that?* I turn over to Padrino, who has a broad grin on his face as he's let down from being pushed back against the wall. The rider spins his magnificent steed around and charges toward Lorcan.

Lorcan turns quickly to Padrino and jabs his scythe into his stomach. Madrina falls to the floor, letting out a loud, shrill scream. The rider disappears back into the portal as if nothing is holding him here any longer. Ava lets out a shriek of anguish and runs to her grandfather, followed by her aunt. I turn to Lorcan.

Rage emerges from the pit of my stomach. I take out my dagger and channel that energy up my arms and out through the tip of the blade. Fuck neutral force and fuck anything else. The dagger is the quickest way. Pain shoots up my head, my skin opening up as the rest of my horns grow out fully. I don't care.

A gurgling sound comes from Padrino, followed by a faint whisper, "No, Addison. That is not the way."

I keep my eyes on Lorcan, whose head is tilted back. His lips curl in disgust as he stares at my transformation. With brute force, he fights my powers and grabs my wrist. I yank back but his death grip tightens as he grabs onto my dagger with his other hand.

Rage forces itself up from the pit of my stomach, my mind losing concentration of what I'm holding. Vines break free from the walls and grab onto Lorcan, pulling him back. I blow wind out of my lungs and send an icicle-shattering hole to open up in the wall behind him. A portal opens up within that ice and I push at the air with my hands. He lets out a single yell as the wall swallows him whole, taking my dagger with him.

I let out a sigh of anguish as I turn and run toward the front door, where Padrino has fallen. Madrina and Ava are crying over his body. I place a hand on his wound but there's so much blood, I don't know what to do.

"Addie, we need a hospital."

"Yes, we need to take him in." My gut sinks as I say it, knowing that no hospital could possibly be functional right now. Padrino has a tear in his eye as he looks up at Ava and Madrina. He grabs a hold of my hand and squeezes it.

"Padrino, I'm so sorry. This is all my fault."

"Shhh … No, it is not."

"I'm sorry. I couldn't find my balance, I used dark magick again. I didn't have time, and I didn't know what to do."

Ava's voice grows dark. "Did you kill him? Did you kill Lorcan?"

"No, I can't kill a reaper. I sent him through a portal."

"How did you do all that?"

"I don't know, I just did. I thought I needed my dagger, but I guess I don't anymore … He took my dagger." Air catches in my throat. Lorcan has the dagger.

"A–Addison …" Padrino whispers.

"Yes, Padrino? What do you need? Anything?"

"You must raise your powers … neutral …"

"But how?"

"By letting … go … of … that … anger …"

"I'm trying, Padrino … but it's hard."

"Start … with … forgiving … your brother …" Padrino's head falls to the side.

"Oh my God … Grandpa?"

Padrino closes his eyes. I check his pulse and my lips tremble as tears swell. "He's gone. I'm so sorry."

⋈

We help carry Padrino's body to the couch so that he wouldn't be on the floor. Madrina covers him with a blanket and sits down to pray by his side.

"Ava, I—" I swallow and close my eyes. Ava hugs me.

"I know," she says. "This wasn't your fault."

"Yes, it is. I never should have come here. Even my brother told me not to. I should have listened." My voice breaks as I take in shallow breaths. Clenching my fists, I move away from Ava's embrace.

"You should go," Madrina says, standing up. My lower lip trembles as I see how Madrina is looking at me. I don't blame her. This is all my fault. I take a deep breath and nod. Ava lowers her eyes and becomes silent.

"Before I go, who was that man who came down from the portal?"

"That was Chango," Madrina says. "Padrino's saint and protector. He must have called him to protect us and then left when Lorcan stab . . . " Madrina's voice trails off.

I take one last look at where Padrino is laying and a tear rolls down my cheek. I place one hand on Ava's shoulder and squeeze it. "I will stop Lorcan if it is the last thing I do."

Ava rubs her eyes and follows me to the door. "Wait."

I stop. "Yes?"

"How? What are you going to do?"

I pause, looking down at the floor. Honestly, I'm lost. I don't even know where Dax is nor how to call him. But one thing is certain. I'm angry as fuck. I want to kill Lorcan, but don't possess the necessary tools to do so.

"Are you going after him? Like, by opening a portal?"

I don't budge.

"Be careful," Addison. I don't want to lose you, too," Ava says.

"That reaper isn't the one you should go after," Madrina

says as her voice echoes through the house. "Vengeance isn't what Padrino would have wanted."

"Okay then, what do you suggest I do?"

"How did all this start?"

I blink. "With Lucifer using Azazel as a scapegoat for his plans."

"As crazy as this sounds"—Madrina stands up and walks over to me—"that is whom you should go after. But not to fight, that's a losing battle. To bring him down and make things right." I hold my breath. She didn't see the way Lucifer manipulated Azazel, manipulated me, and then left me in charge of his prison without a care in the world.

"There's one problem with that, Madrina. I have no idea where to even begin to find Lucifer. And with a god or demon god of his magnitude, I don't stand a chance at getting near him."

"Well, I don't believe that for a second, and neither would Padrino."

I tilt my head back.

"He sought you out for a reason, perhaps with ill intent, or perhaps not. It doesn't matter. What matters is he left you in a position of power, which means you need to take control."

"But I have been taking control. Everything I've learned thus far is from me taking control. I get what Padrino was trying to tell me, I do. But maybe he's wrong about this. If I came from LLAPS, then maybe—"

"Stop it." Madrina grabs my shoulders and lowers her voice. "Lucifer was never a demon," she whispers. "Think. To follow him, you must transcend your powers high enough to reach his."

"But how?"

"What did Padrino say to you before he died? Find your balance."

I sigh. "Okay, I will try."

Madrina nods. "Padrino would be proud. I know you can do this."

I stare into her eyes; hurt, yet strong. "I'm so sorry."

"Go now."

I walk out of the door and listen for the sound of Madrina closing it and locking the latch. I rub the necklace Ambrose gave me between my fingers, then pull the chain hard enough to snap the clasp. *You never came for me. It's your fault Padrino is dead.* I throw the necklace to the grass and walk over it.

I stride to the backyard and peer around the corner. My stomach twists. Skadi broke through a hole in the shed.

Is she really gone? I scan the yard, releasing a few egregores, hoping their essence will guide Skadi back to me. After a few minutes, the egregores run off into the trees, but Skadi doesn't return.

Great, now I'm alone. I bite down on the hurt. My hellhound betrayed me too.

She probably sensed the revitalizers and got scared.

I hope she saved herself. The thought of betrayal brings me to Dax. How am I supposed to forgive him after he lied to me? I must look for Lucifer on my own. He's the only one powerful enough to undo all this.

I make it back to my car and inspect my reflection in the windshield. Two beautifully twisted brown horns with gold veins twining through them stare back at me. Madrina's words echo in my mind. She's right, I can open a portal. I don't need a dagger. It's now or never. I step a few paces back and spread my hands. I close my eyes, envisioning the space in front of my hands as nothing but a frequency between me and another dimension.

Images of dead coworkers shatter my thoughts. My brother lying to me. Skadi running away. Me becoming a demon. Azazel. Then Ambrose.

Padrino's voice echoes in my mind. *This is not the way.*

I open my eyes and yell, bringing my arms down.

How can I find my neutral energy now? By rising above? Easier said than done.

My cloak billows in the wind as I close my eyes again. Focus. A soft wind touches my fingertips. A portal swirls in front of me. My eyes widen. *Was that me?* But I didn't feel any hatred . . .

I look around and take a few steps forward. I touch the surface of the portal with my fingertips. The magnetic pull from the spinning black void reels me in. I take a deep breath and step inside.

A flash of blue light blinds me, and I tumble through a hole as it replaces solid ground.

GRIEF-STRICKEN

AMBROSE

I step out of the veil by Padrino's still body.

Ava jumps up. Madrina screams and pushes Ava behind her.

"What do you want?" she yells.

I lower my head and morph into my human form. Ava drops her shoulders and lowers Madrina's arms from in front of her.

"It's okay, it's Ambrose."

"Addison's Ambrose?" Madrina's voice shakes.

Ava nods.

"I'm sorry to have startled you," I say. "I came because your Padrino asked me to send you a message."

"Padrino? You saw him?"

"Yes, I'm the one who reaped him. He wanted me to tell you not to be sad for him. He's fine and will be watching over you."

Tears roll down Madrina's face. "Even with the way LLAPS is?"

"I promise you he is not in LLAPS."

Madrina sniffs.

"Wait, you were the one who reaped him? You were here?"

I nod, letting out a small sigh.

"Why didn't you stop Lorcan? Addison needed you! We needed you!"

"I–I wanted to, but I was too late. When I got here, he . . ." I look over at Padrino.

"That's bullshit!" Ava spits.

I pause. "I know I deserve that. You wouldn't understand. If I had shown up, things would have turned out much worse. I couldn't give him the battle he wanted. Not yet."

"You could have figured it out. It's your fault my grandfather is dead!"

This house would have gone up in flames had I been here. Everyone would be dead. I lower my eyes. "Let me help with his body."

"No, you're not touching him," Ava hisses between gritted teeth as she moves in front of the couch.

"As you wish, Ava." My eyes flick from her to Madrina and I lower my gaze. "For what it's worth, I am truly sorry I was not here."

Madrina pats Ava's shoulder and takes a deep breath before speaking. "If you want to make things right, go find Addison. She needs your help putting LLAPS back where it belongs, along with all its creatures."

"Believe me, I am working on it. Where did Addison go?"

"She left a little while ago to find Lucifer."

My chest tightens. Damnit, Addison. "She what? By herself?"

"What did you expect, Ambrose?" Ava shouts, veins popping out from her neck. "Have you seen her? She has horns; she's desperate!"

Ava's scream rings in my ears. The only person to ever

speak to me that way was Addison, and even then, it was never as hateful. "You're right. I'll find her." I set my eyes on the couch where Padrino lies covered. Out the window, I spot Addison's car and walk out the front door for a better look. If her car is still here, how'd she leave? A shiny piece of jewelry catches my eye. The necklace I gave her. I bend over and pick it up. The clasps aren't broken. She must have taken it off, and it hadn't fallen off due to an attack. I make a fist around it and close my eyes. *Where are you?*

PURGATORY PRISON

ADDISON

I open my eyes to darkness. I sit up, removing my hood and shivering as I rub my head from the fall. *Where am I?* Cold, short, grey grass covers a grey, wooded forest. Getting up, I dust the dirt off my clothes and screw up my face. Portals are meant to go from one area to the next, but this isn't LLAPS.

I gaze up at the sky. It's dark grey. No hints of purple or blue in it. *How did I get here?* My eyes widen. The blue flash of light. It had to have come from a scythe! *I was ambushed!* Lorcan and his lackeys must have been watching me.

Squinting, I peer through the grey leafless forest, attempting to make out any passageways or creatures. My stomach twists. This must be somewhere else in the astral plane. Somewhere I've never been.

But . . . If Lorcan did this, why not throw me in a cell in LLAPS? For the first time since my transformation, I'm a little glad I have horns on my head. With them, I'm more intimidating than an average human.

Regardless, I can't stay standing here. I'll have to look for a way back. There's gotta be some clues in this strange place. Maybe whoever or whatever lives here can tell me. Hopefully someone or something of benevolence.

I stick one foot out and test the ground. It's firm. Slowly, I put one foot out in front of the other. I don't want to fall into some kind of quicksand or bog. I have no idea what kind of environment this is. Convinced the ground is the same, I speed up a little. As I step deeper into the grey forest, the twisted, bare branches of the trees become denser. Not a bird or animal in sight yet. I'm not sure whether the lack of beings means this place is safe or just as dangerous.

The trees don't rustle in the wind, nor does a breeze pass through my hair. It's dead and still. I lick my dry lips, realizing I haven't drunk water for hours.

I lose myself in deep thought as I walk, not a clue as to how long I've been moving, contemplating what Padrino told me before everything happened . . . before he . . . died. Before I led him to his demise. I never should have gone there.

I swallow my guilt. Maybe my being in this strange, empty place will be good for everyone. The grey skies darken, and I rub my eyes. My legs wobble like I've been walking for miles. Nothing's changed, but it feels like night has hit.

Who knows how large this world is? If I were dropped in a desert, I could be walking for hours thinking it was some abandoned dystopia. Nevertheless, at some point, I'm going to have to stop and rest for the night. Strangely enough, the urgency to find Lucifer has died down. Even knowing all that's happening on earth, it's been pushed to the back of my head, leaving me more at peace. I don't know if that's a good thing or not, but I can use the break. Over to the right,

I spot a big grey tree trunk and plop down. As I sit, the weight of the world lifts from my shoulders. I've never felt so light, so I close my eyes.

I startle awake to the sound of something moving, scratching in the distance. It's pitch black out, and it takes a few minutes for my eyes to adjust. I bring my legs in, closer to my chest, afraid the boogeymen might grab my feet and drag me into the unknown. After a few seconds, my eyes adjust.

A soft glow emanates in the distance, lighting up some of the grey skies.

Footsteps trample the ground. My spine prickles and I gulp. Crap. I'm out here alone and without a weapon. I pat down my cloak, searching for something to protect myself with. Bastard took my dagger too.

What am I doing? I have magick! Ignoring Padrino's words about finding my neutral space, I search for that dark and angry center. I'm in new territory. There isn't any time for experiments.

Maybe it's the fear of being in a strange place, but any loss I felt, any anger I had before, it's . . . gone. Even by envisioning my dead coworkers, I get a wave of despair, but not enough to summon my powers.

I picture Azazel next, but my anger is swept away by the understanding of my new powers. Even with what he did to me. What the hell is this happening to me? Did Padrino really make this kind of an impact? I picture Lorcan next, and my pushing him into that icy portal and doing it because Ambrose had betrayed me. This summons rage for about thirty seconds before something flies past my face. Whatever it is, it hits the tree, missing me by an inch.

Instinctively, I move to the side and duck. Holding my breath, I narrow my eyes, attempting to make out what the hell that was. As I reach toward the bark of the tree, my hand collides with a smooth, long stick. Gripping it, I yank it out, falling backward. I brace myself with my hand and scurry to the back of the tree to hide. I prick my finger on the sharp end of the object and draw a little bit of blood. Holy fuck. It's an arrow.

I hold my breath as I wipe the blood on my trousers and set the arrow down. More noises echo through the trees. My heart pounds and I drop to the ground.

Am I being hunted? Holy shit, I'm being hunted.

What's worse is they must be able to see me, or sense me. Which gives them the upper hand. If I run, they'll shoot me. My skin prickles. Whoever is out there, they waited for nightfall, for an easy target. I'm such an idiot. I should have looked for better cover than this. I got complacent not seeing anyone around, not thinking anyone could be hiding.

Another arrow hits the tree.

Shit!

I keep my back pressed against the tree and stay very still. Carefully, I feel along the ground with my foot, to where I dropped the other arrow. Might be a good idea to keep hold of this, in case I have to stab somebody.

I let my breath out. My heartbeat intensifies as someone approaches. I focus my energy again, preparing to shoot.

Come on, Addison, what's wrong with you?

I had gotten to the point where I could summon rage without thinking about a memory. And I've regressed? That, or completely stopped. I barely feel anything at all! It happened to me even before landing here. At Ava's, trying to get rid of the revitalizers, but that was because I was trying to take an alternate route to my magick. Now that I'm not taking chances, I should be able to do it like I did at the hospital.

Something rattles a nearby shrub, moving closer from a different direction.

Oh snap. Where do I go? I'm going to have to run.

Okay, I'm in a forest. How about some vines to grab whatever it is sneaking up on me? I try mustering up some magick.

Nothing happens.

Oh my god. What if this place is muffling my magick?

Cold, shallow breaths brush against the back of my neck. I gulp. Something growls. Saliva tickles my skin. And I run.

I can't see where I'm going. Don't care. I keep running, lifting my legs to avoid tripping on lifted roots. An arrow hits the side of my cloak and I yelp. I find the next big tree and run to it.

Am I hit? No, it missed me.

Another arrow flies toward me, missing my head by a few centimeters. I duck and keep going. My pulse races. For all I know, I'm leading myself into the mouth of danger instead of running away from it. I move back against a tree, trying to make out anything in the distance even though it's dark as hell. Something rustles. I turn.

My heel hits a root and I fumble to catch my balance. Falling backward, I land against something large. I gasp, then clamp my mouth shut. Spinning slowly, I face a rock. I pass my hand along it. It goes back pretty far. The farther back I walk, the more distant the soft glow of the horizon becomes. I think I'm in a cave.

I probably shouldn't dwell too far in. Something may be living in here, or I could fall down a hole. I squat against the wall, waiting for footsteps or whizzing arrows. A shadow runs past, and I duck, pulling my hood over my face and aiming the arrow with one hand. When the sound fades, I crawl back until I reach another large rock, crouching behind it. The shadow comes back with someone else, holding a torch lit by a green flame.

Green fire? What kind of place is this?

I peer at them between a gap within the rock and cover my mouth. They're tall, with tight grey skin. Black tribal tattoos cover their bodies, and they have hooves instead of feet. One says something to the other, and when they turn to look into the cave, it's with glowing white eyes and long, pointy teeth.

I press my lips together and cover my nose and mouth, terrified to make any noise. The one on the left says something sounding like a growl mixed with words and walks off. The other creature peers into the cave until his gaze lands in my direction. I'm growing blue in the face but would rather die of suffocation than be eaten by one of those things. Something calls to it and the creature lets out a loud raspy noise, swings his torch, and puts out the green fire. As it walks away, I exhale.

After a few moments, no one else passes by. Maybe they figured they lost me.

It's probably best I stay here for the night. Question is, how long does night here take? It might be a good idea not to fall asleep, should those things come back. Which they might, given that I was so easy to find before.

I swallow. Why didn't they come in? I look behind me, but there's only darkness. I sink back against the cave wall. My only option is to stay put until I can see better. I need to stay awake. I cannot under any circumstances fall asleep.

The silence of the night engulfs my senses and pretty soon, I can't tell the difference between the quiet of the location and the quiet of being asleep.

OPERATION ORDER

AMBROSE

I stand in the courtroom facing the Reaper Council, Dax, and Deacon on either side of me.

"LLAPS is a mess," one reaper says.

Deacon holds out her hand to calm them. "We have a plan."

"A plan? Look around you, there are about sixty of us left. Hundreds of reapers have joined Lorcan. What do you intend to do?"

"What have you done to stop him?" calls out another reaper, and the crowd murmurs.

"Ambrose, you need to tell them something," Deacon mutters. "The more we stall, the more they'll start to think you're not capable of the job."

"Deacon's right," Dax adds. "But don't tell them your entire plan. We don't know who will turn around and run to Lorcan with information."

"I have an idea," I mutter under my breath. I step forward and clear my throat. "Listen to me!"

The crowd's protests grow.

"Quiet!" Deacon's voice booms through the court.

"Thank you, Deacon." I turn to face the reapers. "First, I want to thank every single one of you. Lorcan and a lot of our fellow reapers have betrayed us and Lorcan has been commissioning demons to steal souls from humans before their time."

Everyone gasps.

"He has condemned me for being a rule-breaker when he himself has broken the greatest rule of all. Killing humans, using demons to do it, and all for the sake of creating his own army to rule LLAPS. Lucifer left a portal open, and instead of uniting with us to establish peace, Lorcan took advantage of the change in leadership. My change. Me being Judge. He hates it, and he wants the seat for himself." I let the room grow silent for a second. "If you ask me, that act of hypocrisy is even more human-willed than my relationship."

The crowd nods, staring at me with hollow eyes.

"How do we know you're not just saying this stuff because you want to change LLAPS to carry on your relationship?"

"That's a good question. You have no reason to trust me; I was rogue once, after all. But all of you saw the Judge's scythe choose me. And has it ever been wrong? I want you all to know that you, the High Council of Reapers, are my number one priority. And I have ended my relationship. But not because I'm against it, because I want to focus on bringing us back together. Fixing LLAPS and our council."

More reapers sigh and start talking again. Deacon clears her throat, and they silence. "Lorcan has turned so many against us. Dividing us so he would have the upper hand."

"We're severely outnumbered," one reaper says from the back row.

I nod. "Yes, we are. But fear not! I have a deadly weapon. One he will not see coming."

"What is it?" someone says from the crowd. "Yeah, what's the weapon?"

"I will not speak of it, but I do ask you to trust me on this. I have to keep its secrecy away from Lorcan finding out. When the time comes, you will all see."

A few of the reapers sigh and grunt while others turn to talk. "He has nothing planned," I overhear one of them say. One of them stands up. "So, what do we do?"

Deacon moves forward. "Now, we prepare for battle. Meet in the LLAPS field where the portal had opened in ten minutes."

Deacon turns to me and Dax as reapers get up from the stadium seats and walk out.

Dax broods. "Uh, Ambrose? Tell me you weren't bluffing."

"I wasn't bluffing."

"Well, maybe a little," Deacon says.

I snap my gaze to her. "What do you mean?"

"We're trusting that he's coming."

"Trusting that who's coming?" Dax says.

"I'm confident Orlando and Crowley succeeded after you rescued them."

Dax raises an eyebrow. "My dad? He had to be rescued? What the hell went on?"

"Yes, your dad's spirit was here."

Dax sighs. "Yes. I know, he left his body looking for Addison. You told me he was safe."

"And he is, now. Lorcan had found them."

"And you didn't tell me? I'll kill that sick son of a—"

"But I found them in a cell and safely escorted them

out," Deacon says. "They told me of their plan and it was a good one. One that *if* they succeeded will save us all."

Dax clenches his jaw and raises one eyebrow. "*If?*"

"We'll check on them through the Akashic waters," she assures him.

Dax turns to me. "Anything else you want to mention about this plan of yours?"

"We need to train and wait. I've studied Lorcan's strategies. He has attacked, yes. But I have seen how he goes about it. Give him some space and make him think we are retreating. Then, we attack."

SON OF A DEVIL

ADDISON

"Shit! When did I fall asleep?" I wake up in a panic, my neck aching. The skies are a bit lighter than before, but still grey. The time of day doesn't seem to cause a significant change in light, but it's enough to see by. My stomach roars and my head spins. I can't remember the last time I ate anything. I hope I don't puke. Even if I found something resembling food around here, it could be poisonous.

A loud shriek makes me jump. I edge near the entrance of the cave, cautious not to be seen. An engine roars around the corner. Pressing myself to the wall, I peek around it.

I shoot back as a motorcycle speeds through the forest and disappears.

What the hell was that? A green fireball chases after it, disintegrating as it hits nothing. I gulp and snap my attention to where the fireball came from. Someone stands between the trees, but I can't make them out. I step away from the wall for a better look, but they're walking away. What are the chances they're friendly and can tell me something about this place? Like, how to get out. Or how to find food. The grass crunches beneath my feet as I move closer.

A cloak, akin to mine, sways in front of me. That's a bit weird. My mother made me this cloak.

The figure with my cloak pauses as I take a few steps. She shrieks a high-pitched, angry cry and throws another fireball. As she turns, her cloak drops, revealing her face and two horns sticking on the top of her head.

I gasp. What in the h— The girl looks exactly like me!

"Woah, who are you?"

The girl's eyes narrow and black out. A gold glare sweeps over her horns as she lifts her hand and a green fireball appears.

"No, wait . . ."

The girl aims the fireball and throws it. I dodge to the right and trip over my own feet, breaking the fall with my elbows. I scramble to get up when one of the beasts from the previous night comes out from the woodworks. It looks around and grunts to itself as if pissed off to have just been woken up.

I slowly but swiftly move back on the ground, trying to not make a sound as I stand. The creature cracks its neck and then stops to stare at me. Its white glazed eyes are big. You could almost see clouds moving inside of them as they peer into me, inside my soul. I look back to see where the girl, my apparent twin, went. The creature springs on its hooves and jumps high into the air. My knees tremble as I twist my body to run. Not that there's anywhere to run to!

Something scuffs the ground beside me. What was that? Please don't let there be two of these things awake . . .

The creature lands right in front of me, snarling. I stumble back and reach for the arrow inside my cloak but fall short. I must have left it inside the cave. A large set of twisted horns pops out from behind a boulder, paired with glowing white eyes. As it emerges into view, my jaw drops. It's a giant fucking goat.

The girl turns and backs away from me. My eyes widen. The goat charges it at full speed, its horns menacing and pointing straight forward. I fall back against a tree, not knowing where to run. A second passes before realizing I'm holding my breath and let it out as the creature takes off again.

That *thing* is afraid of goats? A big goat, but still. I turn to the goat, unsure if it had purposely saved me or if it's just hungry for some tall ugly creature and is going to try and eat me.

The goat huffs at me and I still. I've heard of billy goats killing people, but what could a goat with glowing white eyes from a different dimension do? If those creatures hunting me are scared of it . . . I gulp.

The goat trembles. A soft glow emanates from its body and it starts to change form. I don't know whether to run or stay to find out how this is going to turn out. I watch in awe as the goat transforms into a man. The aura around him sucks back into his body and my mouth drops open.

No. Not him.

Rage welcomes my hungry pit, replacing the solace I had felt earlier. Before the beasts. Before being hunted. The reason for all my anger and troubles is here, with me . . . as a goat.

". . . Azazel? How . . . what the hell? I thought you were dead?"

"Not dead, but I might as well be. I'm stuck in this hell hole."

"Dare I even ask?" I stammer as his dark eyes bore into mine, as they once did down in LLAPS. I force my gaze into them. He's . . . naked. Probably because he used to be a goat. And it's not like it's the first time seeing him . . .

Ugh! I shake away the memory. "W–what happened to you? One minute you were going for the Judge's scythe and then . . . you vanished. I thought you died.

"It transported me here instead." His gaze flicks to the side, then back up at me. "My father . . . what did he do after I vanished?"

I purse my lips. What did he do? Tried to make me Queen of your hell hole and then dipped. "He left," I say instead. His dark eyes loom over me, his expression unreadable.

To my surprise, my rage dies down. I should be feeling enough rage to summon my power. It's this place. It's snuffing out my emotion. "I haven't been able to reach any kind of emotion since I got here. How did you transform yourself into a goat?"

"I didn't intentionally. This place brings out who you are. And since I was a demon, it turned me into the thing I hate most about myself, the scapegoat Silas turned me into."

Silas? Who is he talking about? The way he turned to the Judge . . . such rage . . . something tells me there's a lot more to his story than I know. "So how come you didn't get stuck that way?"

"Because I am still an alchemist. It took me a while, but I managed to learn how to turn myself back at will. Until I realized those things out there hunt demons and I was safer as a goat."

"Why are they afraid of goats?"

"I don't know." He shrugs one shoulder. "I think it's because they've never seen one before. They look for the human-demon appearance. These things are tribal, but they feed on evil."

"But . . . I'm not evil."

Azazel smirks. "No? Nice horns, Addison."

My scowl deepens as I touch the pointy tip of the twisted left horn on my head. "How does this make me evil? *You* made me this way, and then I took what you taught me to do *good*." Damn well I did!

Azazel folds his hands. "And what good exactly have you done so far? Catch me up."

"I've tried to save prisoners that escaped LLAPS from the reapers."

"Kill or harm any demons while you were at it?"

I quirk a brow, not flinching. My lips purse and then I let out a sigh.

"Thought so. You need to win them over, not hurt them. They want someone to follow. I left them to you for a reason. I believed you would be compassionate about the unwanted and unworthy."

"But why would I? Why did you ever think that?"

"You know why. You've always been different. Seen the world differently."

"Because of my demon blood?"

Azazel nods and I roll my eyes. He licks his lips and looks me up and down.

"There's something different about you," he says slowly, holding out a hand and inching it toward my belly, pressing close to me. Too close.

"What are you doing?"

He smells my hair, and I flinch, tilting away from him. I don't want to be near him or feel his . . . essence. Had we been someplace else, I'm sure I'd be disgusted. But to be honest, I think I'm far too nauseous and hungry to carry on feeling anything else. And tired. So tired.

A soft chuckle escapes his throat and a dimple creases the left side of his face. "So beautiful."

"What is it?" I ask, shaken.

"Did you know?"

I do. I've been in denial, but I do know. And I don't need a test to tell me. But I stay silent, looking back at him, my breath shallow. I don't want it to be true.

"You're pregnant." The words slide off his tongue in a gentle, almost serenading tone.

"H–how do you know for sure?"

"I can tell." He lifts his hand to my face, touching my cheek. I wince. A demon of his stature would be able to know. It's confirmation. But exactly what I don't want to hear. I inhale and he drops his head but watches me.

Movement shakes the trees. "Shh," I say. "It might be her again."

"Who?" He looks toward the trees.

"My look-a-like. She tried to kill me earlier before the creature came back. Did you see her?"

Azazel smirks. "Oh. I didn't see her, but I know who you're talking about. She won't hurt me."

I scoff. "She won't hurt you, but she will hurt me?"

"Well, she probably thinks you want to kill her. She's most likely trying to stop you before you do."

"Why the hell would I want to kill *her*? I didn't even know of her until today! And why does she look like me?"

"Because she *is* you, Addison."

"I mean, she looks like me . . . But how?"

"Don't you see what this place is? I came here as a goat and had to relearn who I was to be able to transform back. You landed here powerless, left to defend yourself with primal resources. And now you see the evil version of your-self, throwing fireballs."

"So, is she . . . who I will become?"

"Maybe."

"Or, who I'm afraid of becoming?"

"Bingo."

I step back, running my fingers through my hair. "One thing I don't get is I was pushed here by a reaper named Lorcan. He wants me dead, so why would he send me to a place where I can hone my skills?" I don't know why I'm still here talking to him. I should leave. Not that I have anywhere to go. And he would follow me. Fuck.

"He probably thinks you'll get hunted and eaten. Or you'll get killed by your evil self. Not even reapers know how this place works. So, joke's on him."

I tilt my head back. "Okay, so how did you learn to transform back?"

"I accepted who I was."

"I already accept who I am."

Azazel smirks. "I accepted who I was . . . completely."

I sigh. "I do!"

Azazel mimics my sigh. "Look, you can be stubborn if you want and I can go back to sleep. Out here, I have no reason to help you." Azazel turns to walk back toward the cave.

My lips part. So, he'd leave his unborn child? "Fine. Go." My heart thuds as I watch him walk away. I mean, it's not like I'm planning on keeping it anyway. A demon baby. Azazel's. I swallow a heavy sob. Regardless, I can take care of myself out here . . . Aw, fuck. "Wait."

Azazel pauses.

"Can you tell me what you mean? *Completely*?"

"Ask yourself this. Have you reached your full potential?"

I stay silent. I still need to find my neutral place—whatever that means.

"What's keeping you from doing that?"

"I guess I haven't forgiven my brother for something."

"Okay, good start. Resentment is a weakness. What else?"

"I don't know what else. But . . . I haven't let myself think about the fact that I'm carrying your demon spawn."

Azazel snaps his mouth shut and leans in until he's inches from my face. "I am sorry for the way I did that. I'm used to getting what I want. I know that's no excuse, but you will have everything. You and our baby won't need for anything."

"No, I won't. Because I'm not keeping it," I spit.

He laughs. "You know that's not true."

"Now you're in denial. Your spawn is probably evil. I can't keep it even if you hadn't deceived me the way you . . . did."

His face goes rigid. "Evil? Do you really think I'm *evil*, even after everything? Knowing where I come from?"

Yes. But I don't say it aloud.

"Even after what I taught you? Is that why you went off saving prisoners?"

I bite my tongue.

"That baby is innocent, Addison. And remember. Half mortal. It can be anything it wants to be."

A tear wells in my eye.

"And besides," he laughs. "There's no way to abort a demon baby, even a half-demon child. You can kill yourself trying, and it will still be born."

Holy fuck.

"In any case, that's not why you haven't reached your full potential."

My eyes flick up to him. I couldn't mutter a word even if I tried.

"There's an evil version of yourself out here trying to kill you before you kill her first." He continues, "What does that tell you?"

I clear my throat. "Th–that I'm still afraid?"

"So, go and kill her."

"But isn't that evil?"

"Not here. She isn't real. Even though she can physically hurt you. Out here, our deepest fears come out to play and become real. But if you kill it, you kill only your fear, allowing you to rise above. You should know this by now."

"So, like the mental plane? Or the prisons? Yes, I think I'm finally starting to get it. But if I can't use magick, how do I kill her?"

"Yes and no. She isn't an egregore. She's like a part of yourself you need to get rid of to move on. Egregores are more like footprints our emotions leave. They all emanate from souls though. You can't use magick because your deepest fear and angst are in your way out here. Until you kill her, you won't be able to use it."

I snap my head toward the cave. "I got it." I sprint back to my old hiding spot and retrieve the arrow.

"Perfect," he says. "Just be careful of the creatures here. They should be asleep, but they will wake up if there is too much noise."

I nod.

Azazel looks at me. "By the way. Where is the dagger?"

My cheeks burn. "Lorcan grabbed it from me before I pushed him through a portal."

The corners of Azazel's eyes redden. "Are you kidding me? Do you have any idea the power this reaper now holds?

Forget the Judge's scythe. He'll be like a god! How could you be so reckless, Addison?"

"I don't need to explain myself to you. A lot happened. He took it from me and I couldn't stop him."

Azazel wipes his face.

"Hey, this is your fault. All of it. Lorcan took the dagger because of you. I'm here because of you."

He straightens himself up. "You're right."

"What?"

"What? I can admit when I'm wrong."

"Help me get back. You know how." I cross my arms.

"I told you how. I can't beat her for you."

"Yes, but I need you to help me do it." I can't believe I'm pleading with Azazel. I grunt and grab his shoulder as he turns away. "Wait, please, I can't do this without you."

"What's in it for me?"

"Umm . . . your child's well-being?"

"Let's be clear here, Addison. The moment you give birth, I'll know. And I'll be coming for it. You can either be with me or against me. Your life is inconsequential to me."

My jaw drops. "That's rich coming from you. You told me you loved me, remember? Was I *inconsequential* then?"

"And then you tried to kill me. Twice." His words are like venom. But it's not like we were ever friends. Seth doesn't count; he was deceiving *me*!

My mouth snaps shut as he spits his words, the little twinkle in his eye when he looked at me being snuffed out. For the first time looking at him, I can see real betrayal in his eyes. I actually hurt him. And from his tone, he doesn't care to be deceived by me again. Looks like we both have something in common there. Never to be deceived again. Yet still. "Yeah, I did. Like you didn't deserve it?"

"Inconsequential," he repeats.

You are fucking evil, you lunatic. "Fine, what is it you want?"

He turns slightly. "A way out. I want to get to HAPS to find my father."

"How do you know he's in HAPS?"

"Trust me, I know. And I, being a full demon, cannot get there by myself. But you can, if you regain your powers."

Then that's where I need to go myself. "Done."

A fireball flies past us and disintegrates when it hits a nearby tree, engulfing it in a green flame.

"Come, follow me," Azazel says. I follow him along the side of the cave to a boulder.

"This should give you good cover."

I press myself between the boulder and the back of the cave.

"Don't be afraid, Addison. Hesitation here will get you killed. Use the rock as cover but be confident, chin up!"

I grip the arrow and point it upward.

"You're holding it wrong. Here." He grabs the arrow and turns it downward before giving it back. "Make a tight fist around the hilt, don't hold it too far away from the point, but not too close either. There, like that."

I practice sticking my arm out.

"Jab it like you're throwing a punch, but with your fist out. It's harder to resist your blows this way."

A rush sweeps over me. I've never trained like this before, but it's sort of fun. I had almost forgotten Azazel commanded a demon army once.

A fireball hits the rock, spurting green flickers of ash by our legs. I peek around the stone, but my clone is nowhere to be seen. From the size of the fireball, she must be close.

"Okay, you've dodged a fireball. Are you going to wait for

her to close you in this corner, or are you going to bring the fight to her?"

I gape at him. "You want me to go out there?"

"Well, unless you can smoke yourself out from here, I suggest you make a move."

"Right."

"The fireball came from there," he says, pointing to the right.

"How come you can see her now and aren't hiding from her?"

"She isn't after me, she's after you. That's how this works."

"Oh, right."

"I didn't hear any movement, so she must still be over there. If she were smart, she would have moved by now, but I doubt it."

"Hey! That's still me you're talking about."

"And you're not very skilled in the art of war, are you?"

"Fine." I dash to a tree as a fireball flies out and hits it. I yell and another one misses me by a hair.

"Don't yell. You don't want to wake *them* up." Azazel walks to my side. "She knows you're hiding here, and you still don't know where she is."

"That's not helping."

A branch falls in front of us, ablaze. Azazel pulls me back, causing me to nearly fall on top of him, coughing.

"She's not going to let me near her." I scurry back behind a different tree.

"She seems to only be using fire."

I screw up my face. This is true. "I think it's because it was the first one I mastered when I freaked out about what was happening to me."

"Use that to your advantage then.'

"How? Do you know of any streams nearby?"

"Not that I've found. You're going to have to outsmart her."

"You mean outsmart myself. How the hell am I supposed to do that?"

"What do you think she's afraid of? If she's mastered all the elements, it wouldn't be water."

I arch a brow. "You said those things out here hunt demons, right?"

"Yeah." Azazel narrows his eyes, a dimple sneaking upon his face. "What are you going to do?"

"Run." I turn and start running from tree to tree, shouting random things. "Hey! Over here!"

"What the hell are you doing?" Azazel calls. He turns back into a goat.

An arrow flies past my nose and I run in the other direction. A fireball flies toward me and I duck, letting it fly past the beast. I dash toward the fire instead of away from it. I beckon to the goat to follow.

Finally, I get a glimpse of the coat as my clone runs behind a nearby tree, waiting for me to pass. I sprint in her direction, ignoring any fireballs being thrown. Azazel circles around the other side of where my clone is hiding. Together, we close in on her.

I yell again, and the girl prepares another fireball. A beast jumps right over my head, landing in front of my evil clone. Azazel charges at him while I take the beast's place, pointing the arrow right at her neck. I inch in, peering into the black soulless eyes of my evil self.

Another green fireball emerges from her hand, but before she shoves it in my face, her eyes shrink.

"I'm not afraid of you," I say. "I am not afraid of

becoming you, because I know this isn't all me. But I accept you."

The black in the girl's eyes disappears. And she puts her hand down. Now, I'm looking straight at myself.

"You still have to kill her, Addison." Azazel approaches from behind, no longer a goat.

I hold the arrow close to her neck and tears form in her eyes. Then, it hits me. She was throwing fireballs because she let herself become so evil, she lost the rest of her magick. And I'm almost there. I can't let myself become this thing. I tighten my fist and jab the arrow into her throat. My clone coughs, blood gurgles out of her mouth as it seeps from her wound.

My hand shakes, and I let go of the arrow. It feels so real. But then, the girl vanishes in a cloud of red smoke.

It's done. I let out a sigh of relief and stand up.

"Well, that's not how I would have done it. But good job. Now, open the portal."

"That's it? I don't feel any different."

Azazel smiles. "Are you sure?"

Looking at the bloody arrow I had used, I let it fall to the ground. A huge weight lifts from my shoulders. No more anger. No more pain. Just like that, I feel like I can forgive my brother for lying to me. I understand why he did it. And why Deacon did it. My eyes flick to Azazel's. I even understand Azazel because of where he came from, how he was treated, as a babe and growing up, only to live out most of his life in a cell. Full of vengeance. And used to getting what he wanted before all that. I don't have to forgive him, but I can forgive myself while understanding him. That makes all the difference. Padrino was right all along. Angels, demons, up, down, it doesn't matter. We're all neutral entities, living with preconceived notions about ourselves, with the power to discover our fullest potential. If we open our eyes and find it. And I no longer fear who I am. "I changed my mind. I do feel different."

Azazel nods. "Ready then?"

"One more thing."

He leans on his other foot. "What?"

"There's one thing I don't understand . . . Why did I have to unlock the elements to gain control of my magick?"

"As a demon queen, your magick is different. You're not a lesser-lower demon with one form of magick. When you transformed, your magick mimicked that of earth. The elements are earth's magick, and LLAPS is a mirror image of earth, despite the tunnels and prisons."

Huh. That actually makes sense. There's water, stone, temperature changes . . .

"Everything you feel and experience in the astral planes resonates with the elements. But Addison . . . it wasn't all about unlocking the elements. It goes back to you accepting and thereby relearning who you are. A demon queen.

I scoff. "I might have the power of a demon queen, but it doesn't mean I'll take the throne."

Azazel smirks. "You may think that, but every time you unlocked a bit of your power, you were one step closer to accepting your role of queen."

I open my mouth to object, but before I can he interrupts, "Shall we get on?"

"Fine." I nod and close my eyes, finding my neutral place. Without any hate, it's easy to forget the emotions I once held on to. I know what I love, but don't need that to summon power either. I summon a beige color in my mind's eye. All of the elements come to fruition all at once.

The fire roars through my veins. Wind blows around me and drizzles of water sprinkle the ground. And the grey ground starts to become warm. I open my eyes, and a strange tingling sensation tickles my palms. A translucent silver stream flows from my hands toward the sky.

The essence of spirit. Quicksilver. The final stage.

The horns on my head retract inside my skull, ready to reveal themselves at my will. I smile as I let it all go and close my fists. All of the changes stop at once. I feel the top of my head with my fingertips.

"Are they gone?"

"Not entirely. You're just in control now. You've become a master of your alchemy." Azazel bows to me.

"Stand back." I hold out my hands and a white shimmery portal opens. Just like that. I don't need to focus my energy, summon any memories. I think of what I want, and it happens. I've finally understood how to reach my neutral place. Magick isn't black or white. Anyone can summon energy from anger or happiness, but understanding the need for balance, and learning to be above it, is a whole other feeling in itself.

I look back at Azazel, who's pressing himself to me. I close my fist holding the arrow and turn, jabbing him in the chest. I know it can't kill him. But he's not getting into HAPS. Where he goes, chaos follows. And Lucifer knows the world is better off with Azazel in here. He falls backward, away from the portal. The look of betrayal on his face is the last thing I see before I step into the gateway of gold and silver swirls, and watch it close him out.

A glowing yellow light blinds me. A tall man stands at the center of it, curled horns protruding from his head.

THE SECRET WEAPON

AMBROSE

Clutching my golden scythe, I walk between the formation of reapers while they train under Deacon's watchful eye, Dax assisting her, flicking between reaper to reaper, fixing their stances, guiding them in combat training. There aren't many of us and reapers aren't accustomed to fighting, but long ago, these scythes were meant for much more. They were created by Azazel, master of many things, including reaping and war.

Someone asks Dax how he can catch himself on fire and control it. I pause and listen in.

"It just happened when I needed it to. I wasn't exactly a weakling when I was alive. I was strong and quick-tempered. When I was protecting the Ashaninka when Azazel cast me out to the rainforest, I found myself surrounded by war and angry at what was happening. I let that anger fuel me, and instantly, I was covered in fire."

I carry on walking. That *is* interesting. I wonder if it happened to him because he used to be human. Or if it could also happen to any of us. Just like I developed empathy, which led me to leadership. And Deacon, long ago, came into some powers of her own. The ability to listen to people's thoughts. We've had conversations like that before, without me having to speak. It has helped us out so far. She has an upper hand against Lorcan. Unfortunately, her skill can only take us so far. She isn't psychic and sometimes there's too much noise in someone's mind.

It's making more sense why reapers have been subjugated to an imprisonment of sorts. Not allowed to know more than what we were given. But this ends now. My army will learn to ascend to their fullest power. There has to be more to us than just guiding a soul this way or that.

I walk over to a high vantage point in front of my legion and clear my throat. Time for a pep talk. Everyone stops what they're doing.

"I know what is to come terrifies you all. But don't let it. Even though we reapers have been around for millennia and very few of us have seen any change, deep within us, we know that nothing is permanent. My predecessor made changes by locking Lucifer and Azazel up, taking control of Azazel's golden scythe, and creating all of us. And now, it's time for another change. You all did an excellent job today. What I saw today was not unpracticed reapers, but reapers who were born with an innate, natural ability to do what you were created to do. To protect the natural order of things." I pause. "You should all be proud of your progress and worry not about our size. I saw the intelligence you could all bring to the fight. Dax has a power that none of us have ever possessed, and he will be here on the front lines with us."

Dax nods at my remark and reapers clap.

"And I've never seen a better leader who can take charge when needed than Deacon. Deacon, I could not have done any of this without you. It is an honor not only to be Judge of the High Reaper Council, but to be able to rule by you, for eternity." I start clapping and others join in.

"Now, let's all go back to our quarters and rest. We don't know when Lorcan—"

Black portals rip the purple sky open. Reapers leap out, landing on their feet. We're surrounded.

Dax backs up next to me, his right arm catching flame. "They're here already?"

I let out a huff and hold my hand out to Dax and the other reapers, calming them down. "Easy everyone, prepare for defense."

Deacon takes over, always ready, and leads the formation as Lorcan makes his way toward me.

"What do we do?" Dax says.

"I expected this."

"You what?"

"Lorcan has been trying to pop up and surprise us. But I was ready. I couldn't risk anyone overhearing, so I kept it to myself."

"OK, good. I'm guessing you mean that secret weapon you promised?" Dax looks to Lorcan's battalion.

"I sure hope so."

Dax shoots me a side glance, his eyebrow raised. "Hope?"

I don't say anything, keeping my focus on the sky. I turn to Lorcan and grip my scythe tightly in my right hand.

"Relax, Ambrose. This is merely a friendly visit," Lorcan says.

I nod. "Is that why you've brought an army?"

"They're here just in case our conversation goes awry. I have to tell you. I saw Addison a little while ago. That bitch has guts."

A fire burns inside my core but I force it down. It's

crucial I keep my cool, lest I risk opening myself up for defeat.

"Full-blown demon. She's evil, Ambrose. Did you know that? Do you know what she did?"

"No, but I'm sure you're going to tell me."

Lorcan snickers. "She was able to open up a portal and push me in. I of course redirected myself to my quarters. But wow, if she can do that to a reaper, what else can she do?"

"She has many talents. And you went after her. Defending yourself is hardly evil."

"Oh, but it's the manner in which she did. Her potential. That's what's dangerous."

"What do you want, Lorcan?"

Lorcan raises his chin as he looks down at me. "Don't you want to know how I retaliated?"

Dax steps closer. I hold my arm out to keep him back.

"Well, let me tell you anyway. She tried to open another portal, and I had two of my allies grab her and send her off into oblivion."

"Where is she?" Dax yells.

"Keep your cool," I mutter under my breath.

"Give up your scythe, Ambrose. And I'll tell you where your girlfriend is."

Deacon looks back at me and shakes her head. "Ambrose, no. Don't do it."

Dax places his hand on my arm. "Ambrose, this is Addison we're talking about. My sister. What's this scythe really worth?

"Dax, step away from him," Deacon commands.

I hold out my hand. "Stop it." Dax fixes his jaw and lets go of me. He narrows his eyes and sneers at Lorcan, lowering his voice to a hoarse, and raspy whisper. "If you hurt my sister, I will kill you."

I push him back. "That's enough."

"You should listen to him, Ambrose. Without me, you'll never know where Addison is. In fact, who knows if she's even survived?"

"Survived? Where did you send her, Lorcan?"

"Oooh, menacing. I like that tone on you, Ambrose. Almost makes me want to let you lead." Lorcan tilts his head as if considering it. "Yeah, no. Hand over your scythe and I'll tell you."

I tilt my head with a half-smile. "I'm afraid I can't do that."

Lorcan snickers. "Then she dies." Lorcan raises his hand, bringing up a dagger with a ruby hilt. "Attack."

The sight of the dagger in his bony hand makes my breath catch in my chest. I glance at Deacon, who is staring back.

An army of reapers points their scythes toward us, surrounding our ranks around the perimeter. They have the upper hand, having dropped from the sky and formed around us. We're caught dead in the center. Dax turns his head to face me and fires up. The skies roar open, and demons jump to the battlefield.

"We are severely outnumbered, and you resisted saving my sister. I hope your plan is worth it."

I furrow my brows. "Dax, I need you to trust me."

Dax gives me one last look before throwing a surge of fire toward Lorcan. He misses as one reaper throws himself in front of Lorcan to shield him. Just as the battle breaks out, a loud shriek comes from the distance.

I look out ahead and smile broadly. From a silver portal in the sky, a white and silver dragon the size of a building swoops toward the reapers on the vantage point. Exactly where I told them to go. Fire flares from its nostrils and disintegrates an entire rank of demons.

Dax extinguishes his fire and his jaw drops. "You've got to be kidding me. Dragons are real?"

I smile and nod.

Deacon runs toward us. "He made it!"

"Best of all, your father came through," I tell Dax, whose eyes have bugged out of his head. "Did you know your father is friends with dragons?" Dax's face twists.

Wind gushes through the field and the dragon's silver, luminescent wings expand as it glides around us and sets a few more ranks on fire.

"Okay, he's really using aggressive force. How many reapers was that?"

"I don't know, but go and make sure he knows not to kill any of ours. I'll deal with Lorcan."

I open a portal and land in front of Lorcan. "Going somewhere?"

"How did you . . . ?"

Grinning, I shake my head. "I have friends."

"This isn't over. You're still outnumbered."

Lorcan raises his scythe, aiming for my head. I block it and punch him in the face, drawing blood. He fires back with a blow of his own. His scythe clashes with mine and the golden scythe lets out a fierce purple light, pushing him back. I don't mean to kill him. But throw him in a cell, I will.

He steadies himself, aiming for another hit. This time, he strikes at my arm, causing me to drop my weapon. He takes out the dagger, the ruby hilt shining in my eye as it retracts energy from the blade of my scythe. My brows knit together. That's interesting. Perhaps he does know what he's doing with the dagger. I lift the hilt and stand, blocking his hits as he forces me to take steps back.

"Two things you don't know, Ambrose."

I don't respond, keeping my eyes on him. Maybe he can kill me with that thing if Azazel created it to replace all power.

"One, there's more than two things that can kill a reaper. And this dagger is the key."

Clashing my scythe with the hilt of his, I kick him in the ribs as he lunges forward. "And the second?"

"There's one thing I noticed about Addison that you don't yet know."

I hold my breath at her name, and he swipes my scythe away as I accidentally loosen my grip. Deadly mistake.

Lorcan hovers over me as my back arches against a boulder we've reached, my feet digging into the ground. He raises the dagger to my neck, the blue streams of the scythe flowing into the hilt of the dagger being pressed against my throat. I refrain from blinking, daring him to use it. Daring him to use her name on his tongue.

"She's pregnant."

What? Before I can do anything, Deacon appears through a portal behind him and wrings Lorcan's neck with her scythe, pulling him away from me. I straighten, not knowing whether to believe him or chalk it up at him trying to wind me up before stabbing me. I lunge forward and grab my scythe from the floor and swiftly move back to aid Deacon.

Lorcan elbows her in the gut, just as the dragon swoops down and aims for him. Lorcan quickly grabs onto Deacon and covers himself, holding the dagger in the other hand. Dragon fire soars down from the sky.

Horror washes over my face as Deacon's bones stiffen, her eyes, dark and sullen, hold a new type of lifelessness as she looks at me. I reach for her as the cracks ripple around her skeleton, turning her to ashes.

"Noooooo!" I drop to the ground as dust and smoke sear my eyes. I pick up Deacon's ashes and look up at the dragon, who is landing on his feet.

"You might have won the battle, but remember, I have the dagger and the souls. This isn't over," Lorcan sneers, disappearing through a new portal.

Dax runs over to us as Deacon's ashes pour out between my fingers. He used her as a fucking shield.

The ground vibrates as the dragon shakes. I glance up at him. A man with two spiraling silver and white horns on his head approaches.

"Ambrose?"

I nod.

"I am so terribly sorry. I was aiming at the white-haired reaper."

My lips quiver but I center myself. Because I have to. I need to be here. And present. "I know. What is done is done. And Lorcan will be back." Dax helps me up and I steady myself, shaking.

Dax, lips parted, eyes rigid, holds me up. We exchange a glance, unable to speak. But we both feel it.

Dax turns to face the horned man.

"You saved us. Thank you."

"It looks like I did more harm than good . . . My name is Evander."

"Dax."

"In war there are casualties," I mutter under my breath. I can't make eye contact. I need to stay collected. For the good of the council. After all, it's what reapers do. It's what Deacon would have wanted.

A bark comes from the distance. Orlando steps through

a portal to our right with Crowley by his side, both following a hellhound.

"Well, that has got to be the funniest thing I've seen all day," Dax says.

"I thought I told you to stay home," Evander scolds.

"What brings you to LLAPS?" Dax asks, hugging his father.

"This hellhound brought me to come find your sister."

I FOUND THE DEVIL

ADDISON

I take a few steps forward, my feet sinking into the soft crystal sand.

"Lucifer?"

The man is cocooned by a yellow glowing light and doesn't even look behind him. My eyes dart back and forth, scanning for anyone else in sight. We're alone. The scent of honeysuckles fills my nostrils as I take in the mountainous view surrounding us. The sky is a bright yellow, so bright I can barely see. Several rivers wind in different directions. If I'm not careful with my footing, I could fall into one of them. My eyes flick back to the demon who seems to be either ignoring me or can't hear me. I'm certain it's Lucifer. HAPS's beings can't possibly have horns on them too, can they?

I take a few extra steps forward, stretching my arm out to reach for his shoulder.

"Lucifer?" I say again, my voice breaking.

"Why have you come, Addison? Not liking being Queen?"

I gulp. I hadn't prepared myself for this moment. "I am

not Queen. And I have retracted my horns."

"Yes, congratulations. You have mastered your alchemy. So, what are you doing here? Go and take command."

"Do you have any idea the mess you made on Earth? In LLAPS?" Even though he's facing the mountains, I can almost see the edges of his lips curl up in a smirk.

"This was your calling for a reason."

"But why me?" I ask, throat dry and heart hammering in my chest. "Why do I have to be the one to do it? I didn't ask for demon blood . . ." I pause, but he doesn't respond.

Sharp horns glow in the luminescent sunlight as he shakes his head. A shiver trickles down my spine. It feels so wrong, having him here. "Please, take the power back. Go back to LLAPS and let me just live my life."

He laughs but it's humorless. "Addison, dear, tell me you didn't come all the way up here to have a pity party?" Finally, he turns, his fiery gaze boring into me. My stomach sinks, but I steel myself and ball my fists.

"I need your help fixing things, Lucifer."

His smile turns snake-like and his eyes gleam like the unforgiving lava of LLAPS's firepit. "I love it when people ask the devil for help. It's music to my ears. But alas, I have taking over to do here."

"W–what do you mean, 'taking over to do here?'"

"Trust me, I'll be back down." He looks me up and down, like a hungry hellhound stalking its prey. Something tells me that he isn't expecting me to stay on as Queen.

"Why not just have gotten rid of me after I let you out? Why not have Azazel be in charge of LLAPS?" Lucifer stays quiet, features twisting in disgust. An air bubble catches in my throat. "You wanted Azazel out of the way. Didn't you? He must have been more of a threat, and I'm not."

"I just wanted to see the look on your face," he purrs,

"when I destroyed your mother's home." He opens his mouth wide, releasing a swarm of locusts throughout HAPS.

*Turn the Page for a
sneak peek of '**Queen of Demons**,' the
fourth book in the series.*

WELCOME TO HAPS

ADDISON

Locusts. Buzzing, swarming, biblical freaking locusts. But honestly, should I have expected anything else? Nothing even grows here, what does he think this'll do? Besides set off an alarm and let everyone know Lucifer is out of his cage. Oh, yeah, I guess that's the point.

Power surges through my arms, flames igniting my palms as an ocean of locusts swarms the yellow sky. In seconds, these giant flying monsters land on my skin, and my fire diminishes. Shit.

"Your power won't work against me, Addison. Go back to LLAPS and do what you're told."

I stumble back, raising my arms above my head and swatting furiously. The deafening buzz almost makes my ears bleed. I open my mouth to speak, to plea for him to stop. If nothing more.

"Lucif—" A locust flies into my mouth. I jolt back, spitting it out. I trip and tumble into the Akashic river.

The current pulls me under. Images of the past, present, and future surface inside my mind's eye—yet I can watch it as if I were watching a movie. But not my past, mankind's.

In the beginning, there was no god, only particles of energy. Fast forward to humankind, and countless battles and wars over survival and territory. Lucifer stands alone on barren soil. He stands tall, semi-clad, with his chest covered in blood. He weeps over the blood loss of his brothers. He speaks, but I can't hear him. I don't have to. Here, I feel his emotions and know what is happening—almost like telepathy.

The image changes to a battleground. Dragons fly overhead, shooting fire. I duck my head. Holy shit . . . Those are definitely dragons! I spin around as metal clashes behind me and I yelp. Azazel, golden scythe in hand, swings it to a tall, ebony man wearing white and gold battle gear. Power sears through the man's arms and Azazel ducks it. Azazel's eyes move to mine and I wince. Can he see me? An arrow buzzes past me and my breath hitches as he catches it midflight before it hits his chest. A sigh of relief leaves my lungs. He can't see me; he was just looking past me.

He aims the scythe toward me, and a purple light zooms out of it. I turn around as a full-blown winged man crumbles to the ground. The other man yells as his friend turns to dust just like the Judge had when Azazel killed him.

A hoarse groan escapes the man's throat as he lunges toward Azazel, making him drop the scythe. Somewhere in the distance a fire blazes and a dragon roars. Azazel flicks his gaze in its direction, quickly kills the man, and makes a dash toward the dragon. I take a few steps to follow . . . curious to know what is happening. The fear in Azazel's eyes when he heard that sound . . . Why are they fighting? A wave washes over me, and the scene becomes fuzzy . . .

Someone grabs my shoulders and pulls me up from the current. A soft pink glow seers in through the slits of my eyes. I blink a few times and a woman with a strong jawline and shoulder-length, curly blonde hair and green eyes comes into view . . . She looks familiar. But . . . it can't be . . . She looks like . . . my mom . . . I gasp and then start coughing. I struggle to sit up on my own and the woman helps me.

"Mom?" is all I manage to mutter.

A warm smile spreads on my mother's face and she nods. She has on gold and silver chest armor and holds a spear in her hand. "Are you okay?"

My knees quiver as I try to stand but I'm literally shaking. "But—I don't understand. How can you be here?" My mother had died of a heart attack when I was sixteen years old.

My eyes land on a half-opened white, stone temple in the distance. White stone slabs cover most of the ground except the flowing streams of the Akashic.

"You're in HAPS, *mija*. The current must have pushed you to the citadel when you fell into the water." HAPS . . . That's right . . . I fell when . . . Lucifer! Memories come flooding back and I shake my head. I'll deal with this later. Right now . . . I meet my mother's eyes.

My nose itches as I try to hold back my tears. "I can't believe this . . ." I wrap my arms around her neck. "I can't believe it's you."

My mom runs her fingers through my hair. "I've missed you so much. Come, follow me inside."

My legs automatically follow her. "Wait—what about Lucifer?"

"Yes, we're taking care of that now. We saw him coming from the Akashic waters. We knew you were here too. Come, follow me. I know you must have questions." Oh, so many questions!

Her body armor reflects off the pinkish-yellow glow of the sky. My brows squint: this is the same armor the men who were fighting against Azazel were wearing in my . . . vision? It sure as hell wasn't my memory. But I did fall into the Akashic, so it makes sense that it was a memory, just a . . . universal memory? Why is my mother wearing armor though? I follow her down a wide, white stone path, passing mountains to the left, to the white and gold marble temple.

Inside, my mom shows me to large white and gold cushions and throws on the ground.

"Where are we?"

"In my quarters."

"So, this is kind of like LLAPS?"

"Kind of, yes. Except this isn't a prison and not so damp and dark." My mother's smile radiates, and I smile back. This is unbelievable. I wish Dax were here . . .

She brings out a small cup of a hot beverage. "It's okay," she says. "You can drink this here. It's only jasmine tea."

I take the cup and the jasmine aroma fills my nostrils and my taste buds as I take a sip. I pause and look at my mom, whose eyes dance.

"Something happened when I fell into the river."

She nods.

"I saw . . ." I struggle for words. "Honestly, I saw so much I don't even know where to start."

"The Akashic holds the DNA of our universe. We use it to scry to look down on the people of Earth."

Huh. "In LLAPS they use it to scry as well, but for other reasons."

"I am aware."

"But there's something I don't get."

My mother nods and waits patiently; I take it as a cue to continue. There's such a calmness about her. Even at the mention of Lucifer being here, there isn't any hint of panic like there would be in LLAPS, or back home.

"In my vision . . . I saw the beginning of mankind . . . but I didn't see a god. Is there one? A god, I mean?"

My mother smiles. "We are god."

"I don't understand . . ."

"People are so consumed by what came before us. It doesn't matter. Humans created stories, and from those stories came power of belief. But magick, or energy, rather"—she waves her hands in the air—"is everywhere. Humans always knew how to call it down. Some just forgot. But we are the ones in charge up here. All of us."

My forehead creases. All of us. Before I get too wrapped up in what that means, my mind drifts to LLAPS. "So, the reapers . . . They weren't in that memory either." Except Azazel holding a scythe, but he didn't feel like a reaper there. But . . . Ambrose and Deacon said they were created to be in charge.

"The reapers were once all human. They just don't remember."

My breath hitches. Ambrose was a human? "They just forgot about it?" Woah . . .

She scrunches her brows. "That's how they wanted it."

Why wouldn't they want to remember? "So then why doesn't HAPS just tell them? Or remind them?"

"Because it's the way things have always been. They have a job to do and they serve their purpose."

My brows raise. "Wait, but Dax . . ."

A slanted frown falls on her face.

"Will he forget he was human too? Will he forget ... about us?"

Her frown deepens. "Inevitably, yes. That's why I wanted him to come up here to be with me. But your father, bless him, called him back to Earth." She sighs. "And now he's a reaper—I did not want this for him."

My stomach churns ... Dax is going to forget who he was, and become some robotic-acting reaper? That'll feel like losing him again. My throat closes. So much has happened though. I'm glad Ambrose had the Judge turn Dax into a reaper ... I just didn't know it meant losing who he is. We thought maybe because he became a reaper after being dead, it would be different. But if the reapers were all human, it wouldn't be different for him ... And now all this has happened ... me becoming a demon ...

I flick my eyes down to my cup. Does my mother know? How much has she seen?

"What's the matter?"

"Mom, I—"

"It's okay. I know everything, *mija*. It doesn't matter." She takes my hands and brings me back down to my seat. "You are still you."

". . . Still me." I quirk a brow. I have to ask. "Did you know about dad?"

"What do you mean?"

"About his demon blood? And how I have it too."

"Not while I was alive, but yes, I know all about the Castillian blood lineage. Demon blood runs deep in his side of the family."

Huh. No wonder the dagger got sent to us then. I guess Azazel's hopes at his escape from prison weren't far off. My mother offers me another calm smile and my eyes narrow.

I'm beginning to find it unsettling how my mother is

acting like there isn't a care in the world. I mean, I want to feel the same calmness, but like . . . she knows I became a demon, and she's fine with it? She was never like this when she was alive. "What about Lucifer loose here in HAPS? You said you guys were taking care of it? Who else is taking care of it? And how?"

"We have an order put in place, like a safety for if and when this ever happened." The image of Azazel fighting men in armor . . . This armor flashes through my mind. The same armor my mother is wearing. They must have been angels . . . My mother catches me inspecting her clothes. So militant.

"What does that mean?"

"Trust me. We are far stronger than he is."

"But mom, what about me? He says I'm Queen of LLAPS. I don't want to be a demon queen. I just want to be me and go home."

My mom tilts her head to the side. "Whatever you choose to do, you have to be true to yourself. Addie, you are special." She reaches behind her and takes something out of a satchel. "I know LLAPS isn't the ideal place to be, but it doesn't have to be that way."

I screw up my face. Not the ideal place to be? Not . . . you need to go home and continue your nursing career? "What are you saying? That I should be Queen of LLAPS?"

"No, I'm just saying that you should follow your heart."

"Well, I thought I was, but it led me to the prison to find my boyfriend. And well . . ." I place my hand on my stomach and look down. My eyes fog up again. Should I tell her? How much does she know? "Things turned out . . . differently." My throat clogs up.

My mother inches closer and throws one arm around

my shoulder, bringing me in. I think she does know but doesn't want to say it. That's okay with me.

"Your life has changed, *mija*. But Addie, you must learn to forgive. I know what happened was horrible, and trust me, he will not go unpunished."

He? Does she mean Azazel? "But now you must make a choice and take charge of the new cards you've been dealt."

I take in her words. She's reminding me of Padrino. What choice do I have, though, really? If I don't save Earth, my home is ruined. Not just for me, but for everyone. But I won't rule LLAPS, I won't. "I just want everything to go back to the way it was."

"Well, maybe it can." She pulls away and shows me a small vial with a purple and gold liquid in it. "Accepting change and moving forward is the only option."

"What is that?"

"If you do not want to take up the mantle, Addie, then don't. We will take care of everything. I had one of our angel alchemists create a potion that will reverse your powers. You won't be a demon anymore and neither will your baby." She squeezes my shoulder and smiles.

My lips part as I clutch the potion in my hands. "I thought this couldn't be undone . . ."

"Anything is possible in HAPS. I figured you would want the choice, but if I were you . . . I would take it. Think of the baby."

I . . . have a choice. I stuff the vial in my pocket and wipe away a tear.

"What about Lorcan?"

"Who's that?"

"The reaper who—"

"Ah yes, we've been watching him too. We will send down our army."

I stifle a gasp. "So, you mean a war?"

"In a way. But they will stand no chance. Think of this as a quick cleanup. I'll have your brother brought up first."

My heart skips a beat. "Wait, can you . . . unreaper him?" Maybe this is a good idea. Fresh start. But what does she mean by a cleanup? What about Deacon and Ambrose? Would I be able to keep Skadi? "Mom, when you say a reset . . . What do you mean exactly?"

Screams shatter the walls and I flick my eyes to the open temple behind me. My mother gets up and runs out to the river. I set my cup down and follow suit. We approach the terrace facing the open plains and my jaw drops. Rivers of blood cover the Akashic waters of HAPS.

What's worse than being crowned an immortal demon queen against your will? Finding out the angel of death impregnated you.

And on top of that? Lucifer left me to clean up his mess while he marches on HAPS. His goal? Destroy everything that ever meant anything to the angels. Including my mother.

According to her, the only way to stop Lucifer's path of destruction is to cause her own. In 24 hours she's going to destroy LLAPS-and everyone I love.

That is, unless I track down the devil and fight him first. Even as an expectant mother, I can never get a day off.

The Judge thinks imprisonment can subdue the Angel of Death. He's an expert at underestimation.

Unfortunately, my ticket to freedom is a screeching, child-stealing demon. Do I dare lull her into submission, just to help my betrayer of a father? Even if it means exposing my deepest, darkest secret?

Desperate times call for desperate measures.

Available in all major eBook stores.

AUTHOR'S NOTE

Boy, after what I put Addison through in *Lying with Demons*, I was sure she was wanting to wring my neck, but now after having written *Blood of Demons*, I know Ambrose is coming for me.

First, I want to thank my editor, Claerie Kavanaugh. Your patience, your godly editing skills, and your friendship are what have kept me from losing my mind. From the depths of the astral planes, I thank you.

To Michael, my husband, proofreader, and Grim House Publishing tech support, without you, I'd lose myself in computer freakouts and technicalities.

Thanks to all the demons in hell for supplying me with inspiration to write this series. A trip to the astral plane never offers a dull moment with you following me back and tormenting me—I mean, telling me your secrets.

And to you, the readers who have read this far, thank you so much from the bottom of my heart. I hope you enjoyed *Blood of Demons* as much as I loved writing it. Addison's journey ends in *Queen of Demons*.

ABOUT THE AUTHOR

Killian Wolf is a Miami, Florida, native who enjoys pirates, rum, and skulls as much as she loves writing about dark magick and sorcerers. She holds a Bachelor of Arts degree in Cultural Anthropology and Sociology and a Master of Science in Environmental Archaeology and Palaeoeconomy.

Killian writes books about obtaining magickal powers and stepping into other dimensions. She lives in England with her husband, a tornado of a cat, and the most timid snake you'd ever meet. When she isn't writing, you might find her at an archaeological dig, rock climbing, or sipping on dark spiced rum while working on a painting.